The Bookman's Tale

Novels by Berry Fleming

The Conqueror's Stone
Visa to France
The Square Root of Valentine
Siesta
To The Market Place
The Lightwood Tree
The Fortune Tellers
Carnival
The Winter Rider
Lucinderella
The Make Believers
The Inventory
The Affair at Honey Hill
Country Wedding
Once There Was a Fisherman
The Bookman's Tale
Who Dwelt by a Churchyard
Captain Bennett's Folly

The Bookman's Tale

by Berry Fleming

THE PERMANENT PRESS
Sag Harbor, New York 11963

Library of Congress Catalog ing-in-Publication Data

Fleming, Berry, 1899-1990
The Bookman's Tale / by Berry Fleming.
p. cm.
ISBN 1-877946-02-8 : $19.95
I. Title.
PS 3511.L4413B59 1991
813'.52--dc20 90-43469
CIP

Manufactured in the United States of America

THE PERMANENT PRESS
Noyac Road
Sag Harbor, NY 11963

To
S.H.B.,
for help unmeasurable,
and unmeasured.

New-minted glint-gleam-shine
up off your thumb
in a rising spin,
not coin-disk or ball but both
at once
and quickly both a rise and fall
to the back of hand —
a win or a lose,
or a neither and both.

— Old Song.

The Bookman's Tale

IF HE CHANGED his eye focus the tall window in front of his chair became a mirror, and without moving his head he could see the planes landing and taking off, crossing at a downward slant or an upward, and also see the passengers at the ticket desk behind him, black and white, patient and fretful, a barefoot boy with a dog on a leash.

Could see out there a corner of "SAN JUAN DE PINOS" set in white shells on a turf bank beyond the shoulders of travelers arriving, walking up the path between the beds of hot-country flowers, the patches of halfhearted grass nursed by revolving sprinklers, between two giant palms with spikey gently bowed trunks and feather-duster tops sliced off by the waiting-room ceiling; and at the same time see the passengers behind him standing dry in the spraying water, walking through the pair of wet palm-trunks, stabbed through their chests now and then by the white arrow of a plane slanted up or down—the out-there stirred into the behind-him, mixing ahead-of with back-of, tomorrow's reverberations with yesterday's drums and yesterday's dancers stomping the bare ground. And yesterday's, "You seek, and you find, but what you find is not what you were seeking," from somebody on the boat, he had already forgotten his name.

The mirrored clock above the ticket counter confused him but his wrist watch (with its gold overlay of wife-daughter-death) showed a clear 11:44, told him again he had a long wait, brought back the hotel clerk and "Yes sir, there's a non-stop flight to Miami at 13:37," and, "No sir" (with a clerk's smile at the impropriety of his question), "I am not familiar with Mrs. Tyner's name before she married, perhaps our Social Director—but she doesn't come on until noon."

Brought back yesterday's Frank Hardly swinging down the deck like a monkey, one hand-hold to the next: "We're doing twenty knots."

"A freighter? Impossible!"

"Ten straight on, ten up and down and sideways."

And yesterday's then-nameless young woman handing him the afternoon *Islander* with, "Ready, Mr. Edward Ray of the *Sunwise Press?"* as if flashing a light in his face out of her obscurity, and seeing himself listed in a corner of the page among "Arrivals & Departures."

And yesterday's wait beside the black road for the bus, forty miles from town, the sun already in the treetops, waiting in the weeds, watching the empty road. Conscious of the others off nearer town in a bright-colored group by themselves, but not looking at them, dangling other thoughts before his mind as you hoped to quiet an apprehensive child—the hours on board the ship, the days, the hour in some port wandering the simmering streets with the others while the ladies did the shops for odds and ends to ornament the Christmas party, making little moves of his knees and shoulders as if to free them from the motion of the ship which they still carried. Waiting, watching the empty road, not alarmed but certainly not comfortable.

Not looking at them but conscious of them there in a corner of his eye if he looked across into the jungle-woods, in a corner of his mind if he looked away up the road, ten or twelve of them, in pinks and greens—a hatband, a belt, a kerchief—five or six men, the rest women and children, moving about on and off the road watching for the bus, watching him, turning away quickly if he glanced that way, talking among themselves in a fast weathered sort of Island-English he could hardly understand, all as black as the road on which he was sorry to think he had ridden hours from town to see "The Castillo."

"Oh, you shouldn't miss the Castle, sir, the *Castillo de San Marcos,"* from the hotel clerk when he mentioned his free afternoon (not mentioning his free evening too—avoiding the thought of it—and his free tomorrow morning, if "Miss Claudia" returned by lunchtime as the voice on her phone said they expected her to). "Only an hour by car, sir, perhaps a little more."

And when he said he didn't have a car, just came ashore, said, "On the *Lindvagen*, yes. Captain Lundquist, yes we know the Captain. Well, you might rent a car. Or take a taxi from the stand out there. The bus goes by the Castle, but I wouldn't recommend the bus, Mr." (glancing at the register) "Mr. Ray."

But, stranger to the Island, not young but still young enough for the idea of a native bus ride to appeal to him over the everyday solitude of a taxi, he took the bus. Seats to spare at first but before it left the city standing room only. Passengers in the aisle swaying from the straps, glancing at him, glancing away and back again as if magnetized by his difference, his pale face, cotton jacket, good Panama hat the only ones aboard. He gave up his seat in a goodwill gesture to a large woman nursing a baby, found a greasy strap and wished he had hired a taxi.

Off at last at a weathered arrow aimed down a path through the woods: "CASTILLO—75yds." Nobody on the path, nobody at the caretaker's lodge—a padlock on the door—and nobody in the courtyard of the Castle until a family of three emerged from under the beautiful egg-shaped arch of coquina stone supporting the stairway, frowned at him without speaking and disappeared toward the only car in the parking area. Windy on the parapet, with a blinding view of the harbor and a far-off ferryboat with blunted ambidextrous ends, white in the sunlight as if to match the white sea birds, the white oyster shell he sailed out into space; alone up there with the restless birds—and wishing he were alone down here, instead of about to be joined by the two men approaching on the road.

"Look like you waiting for the bus, Mr. White," from one of them, halting a few feet away.

He said, "Oh, hello. Yes, I am. I've been over to see the Castle, the Castillo. Quite a place, quite a view. Now to get back to town" (conscious of the tightness coming through his scatter of words and telling himself to ease up, easy does it—nothing premonitory, except possibly the "Mr. White").

No response from the men, no speech; response of a sort in the level-eyed looking at him from where they stood, the younger one a little behind, both with broad-brimmed straw hats browned by the sun and heat to the color of toast, the color standing out against the black woods. "He seems to be running late today, the Holidays, I suppose," just to break the awkwardness of the three of them standing silent in an all but deserted road, his words sinking into the silence like the oyster shell he had sailed out from the parapet. "Does he often run late like this?" sailing out another shell.

Into another silence, the man in front moving a step closer and pushing up the hat brim with the back of his middle fingers. He stopped with his feet apart and said in a tone of explaining what shouldn't have had to be explained, "Mr. White, the bus runs for poor people."

It surprised him—not the fact (after his ride from town) but hearing it stated—and yet the sense of it joined so neatly with the tightness in his chest that it seemed to be only an extension of it in a different medium, extension of the empty road, the cluster of stares from the group, some distance off but as if brought close by their eyes, each pair of eyes aimed at him like blowguns, meeting his own as he looked away searching for how best to reply. And able to find only a noncommittal but delaying, ''There's usually plenty of room, isn't there?'' glancing from one to the other, looking for a sign they admitted there was something they agreed on— and not finding it.

Which the younger man seemed to take as his cue. 'Taxi, mister. That's where you belong to be. How the taxiboy feed his children, you riding the bus? Pale folks ride the taxi.''

Bringing a forlorn grin to Ray's hot face and a stammer that he wished he could find one, glancing about as if one might appear and seeing two men who might have been twins leaving the group and walking toward him. ''Is there a phone round here where I can call a taxi?''

''Telephone!'' from the first man with a sort of laugh and a mumble that he couldn't understand, then, ''All we know, Mr. White, is the bus run for poor folks and white folks don't belong to be on the bus—''

''Here he come!'' in a shout from a woman in the group. ''Come on, Jabish! Johnny-boy!'' all the men turning to look and one of them grumbling, ''That ain't no bus, '' and another, ''That thing coming from town. That woman!''

(the four in front of him like four charred posts of a fence enclosing him, four black uprights blocking a somewhere path, a somewhere river—that he might have dreamed), a woman in a green bandana striding in to brace them, full skirts swaying.

How serious was all this? He couldn't believe they would actively oppose his taking the bus, refuse to let him aboard; and yet they might. Ashamed of the flush he could feel in his face, the tightness in the top of his chest, of the signals to himself (and probably to them) that he was out of his depth. And knew it. He was trespassing, poaching, overdrawing his account, all without precedent in his business experience; how to handle it. Resistance? Unthinkable; one against many, stranger against native—he was like a tourist with no local currency. Help from the bus driver? (when eventually he arrived). Public employee, he would have some authority as to who rode his bus, how they behaved. And take the side of a city-dressed stranger? Of "Mr. White"! He would sit there with his fist on the lever for closing the door, or looking off down the road, or studying the center of his horizontal steering wheel; he would take—or leave—a passenger as these passengers decided.

What to do, then? Were there any choices, any alternatives to turning away, walking back down the overgrown path to the Castle, disappointing these people who seemed to expect him to protest, resist, seemed to be tightening themselves into a mood to counter anything he did. Except walk away.

And if he walked away, what then? Was there a later bus? And if so, when? And wouldn't Mr. White be just as much an outcast? Hitching a ride in a car or truck was hardly worth the thought; the car that was passing—had passed (in the wrong direction)—was the only vehicle to come by in the half hour he had stood there. When he said, as if summing it up for himself, half mumbling, "I need to get back to town," one of the men grunted a sort of laughing, "Some folks walk the road, mister," setting off quick assents from two or three—

As a squeal of rubber told him the car had stopped, pulled his eyes toward it, a blue MG with the top back, in reverse now and halting with a jerk in front of him: "Get in," from the woman in a cotton jacket and white shorts, sliding to the center and flipping the door open with her free hand.

Sorry to have to shake his head but shaking it. "Thank you very much, I'm going the other way—"

"Get in!"

They didn't understand and he pointed toward the town. "I'm going—"

"Get in!" from the man, adding two short revs of the motor for underscoring it, and he sank into the rumpled linen covering the leather seats, the driver zooming away with an MG "zoom" mellifluous to his burning ears, and he was saved—young people, or young to his fifty-eight, pale hair in tangles from the wind, dressed for tennis (or cricket, strange bats in the folds of the top), the woman with a canvas shoe at each side of the stick shift. He said (after catching his breath—trying to hide his having lost it), *"Deus ex machina,"* which clearly meant nothing to either of them but reminded him of the rest of it and he added, *"Apollo appears from above with Helen,"* which pleased the woman.

And pleased himself for remembering it, helping to loosen the tensions still lingering from his roadside defeat—brought back for a moment as they halted at a crossroad to let the bus go by then turned off through a forest of bamboo toward the harbor. The man said something about ''certain elements'' liking to ''keep them edgy. Somebody should have told you,'' as if understanding he was a visitor, leading him on to explaining a little about the freighter and seven days down from Tampa, no time for much of it even if he had been inclined to talk, the man braking with a sliding scratch on the gravel at the foot of wooden steps up to a porch across the front of a cubical house on head-high stilts, windows all open, sashes hinged at the top.

''Give me ten minutes to change and I'll run you in,'' gathering up racquets, cricket bats, towels, a folded newspaper in a rubber band, Ray protesting he would call the hotel for a taxi if he could borrow their phone: ''There's a taxi stand at the door,'' the woman adding with a little laugh, ''Yes, 'Twenty-two taxis facing west.'''

''No trouble,'' from the man. ''I'm taking a plane in an hour. I'll drop you off. *Princess Ann?*''

''Well, thank you. That's very kind of you.''

And the woman—Ray's daughter's age—seated him on the porch with a bottle of welcome Scotch and some ice cubes in a bowl, pointed hospitably at binoculars hanging from the back of a chair and vanished on rubber soles; leaving him facing a sun-streaked view of the bay and, as his eyes grew quiet, of a far-off vessel headed out that he took to be the *Lindvagen* though he realized he might not know her from such a distance, and from the side—only knew her from within (as you may know someone so intimately you forget how she would appear to a stranger), the passengers now down to five, the Captain now shorthanded (possibly promoting the steward until he reached New Orleans again), the door to a cabin in splinters and needing to be replaced—

The ship then changing course to show an ideogram on the smokestack that became a hammer-and-sickle through the glasses as if to warn him against making flash assumptions; such as assuming tomorrow's Claudia would be the one he knew—not a word between them for half a lifetime.

And none expected for the other half. Then four inches in the *Times:*

WALTER MOTLOW, IN AFGANISTAN

Veteran newsman . . . helicopter . . . gunfire in the Chagai Hills . . . Mr. Motlow, according to sources at the left-wing daily . . . to investigate charges of chemical weapons . . . .

He is survived by his wife, the former Claudia Baird of Austin, Texas, and two married daughters . . . .

(no children when last he saw her, now grown up and married—and no doubt divorced, in the modern sequence), memories crowding into his head, the trivial with the unforgetable: "They mowed the wheat below us yesterday, what a glorious smell!" (writing from North Carolina one October—Mot reporting on the union organizers in the textile mills for the *New Republic*); overhearing, before he knew her name, knew only the back of her shoulders over the edge of a sofa, stiff black hair bunched out an inch above a soft white collar, "You're going to the mountains by *bus*!" from some man sitting beside her, unthinkable as a way of getting there.

"Oh yes. My husband needs the car."

"God, you mustn't do that. If you wait until Tuesday I'll take you, I have to be in Asheville on Tuesday."

She silent only a second or two, then, "Tuesday? Tuesday's fine. Thank you very much," jealousy rising in him like a blush though he didn't even know her name, had only come close enough to notice that the laces in her brown shoes were tied with the bows falling front to back (months later showing her how to reverse the tying and send them right and left—having faced the same problem himself and taking it as a sign of compatability). Remembering, later, trying to deny the sense of completeness he felt in her presence, in the very awareness of her existence even when she was not present, refusing to hold with such sentimentality as that she could reinforce his faith in himself, his hopes for himself, could "stop the whirlwind, balk the elements"; and yet unable to deny his feeling of their affinity, the "fit" of their piano-violin difference—telling her so once in of all places a New York taxicab, she looking at her hands. Or at her "hand," at how she should play it?—

Shocked by the sudden weight in his lap, still

on edge from the roadside minutes; it took him an instant, not to see the cat but to adjust to the indiscriminate friendliness of another blue-eyed Siamese taking welcome for granted—after nearly a week of the freighter's gray-spotted Kristine and her serpent hiss for one and all except the first mate who fed her, following him, not close like a dog but springing along behind, rail to cleat to stanchion to pink Florida lumber lashed head-high between the forward bulwarks and offering a broad sundeck for Mrs. Sarah-Wesley Ackworth and Cousin in bikinis until they caught on this was world-class heat and not to be trifled with.

Appearing beside him one velvet morning, taking welcome for granted like the Siamese—one of them (Sarah-Wesley, he thought, not yet at home with names)—he with arms on the hot rail watching the birds like white kites on strings about to dive out of control, gazing at the black cable tailing out behind them trolling for their speed and progress. At the churned-up wake as it settled back to quiet; like anguish quieting with time and distance—the truck without a driver rolling toward them off a slope in the sunshine, gaining speed, rolling unbelievably into the other lane, the coming car swinging out to avoid it, striking them from the front as the van struck from the side, her side, changing his life in an instant, wife broken and in a week mercifully dead, he on crutches for half a year, on crutches of a sort to this day. And seeking a miracle cure next week in San Juan de Pinos (his Pilgrimage to Lourdes)—

"Penny for your thoughts, Eddie," eyes steadily on his face as if not so much to see him as to see if he saw her, bringing back the young clubwomen at home and their cookbook the Press had been publishing for them; and the "few words" they asked of him for an Introduction. "I was thinking of the 'few words' I once wrote for a young ladies' cookbook. They didn't like them."

"Maybe I would?"

"'I sing the merry, merry maidens, / Lithe and blithe of limb and look, / One in girth, in coif, in cadence—'"

"I don't think I do."

"'—Girdled here as if to cook. / God rest ye, little restless lasses, / Plunging ankle-deep in life, / God save your insulated chassis, / Daring now the paring knife—'''

"I would have pared *you* , Edward! Cut you up in one-inch cubes and—"

"'Oh, dabble, dabble, little femmes, / Unleavened in the midst of leaven, / Hang your aprons—'''

The steward announcing lunch with his hand bell on the deck behind them—as he had announced dinner on their first night out, mid-afternoon it seemed, swinging his bell at precisely five-thirty and showing them into their white dining room-living room; seating them at a bolted-down table, four on a bench under a shelf of barricaded paperbacks, the others across in bolted-down chairs, leaving the head and foot for the Captain and his wife who might dine with them or not "depending on wind and weather and the usual temperamental behavior of a cargo ship."

Appearing quite promptly that first evening, a bony man of forty-five with straw-colored hair (home-cut) plastered damp against skull and showing a sort of beaten path round the sides and back where the band of his cap had spent so much time. He made a polite try at connecting faces and names on a card in his hand and signaled with it at the steward to begin serving. "Mrs. Lundquist will not be dining with us but sends her greetings."

When they reached their not-unexpected dessert of white icecream and chocolate sauce he refused his with a contemptuous flat-of-the-hand to the steward, who seemed prepared for it and refilled his coffee cup instead; he pulled it in front of him, fished out a pipe with a charred rim that suggested the smudged top of the *Lindvagen's* smokestack and settled down to making his passengers comfortable as if on Standing Orders from the Home Office. He said it was the custom on his ship, if agreeable to everybody, to tell stories of an evening, take turnabout in relating some significant event that had happened to them.

"Or almost happened. Or," gold edging to his front teeth showing, "that you wished *had* happened,"—stirring up some "Ohs!" and "Ahs!" among them, used to talking all at the same time and with a comfortable inconsequence. But alternate diversion seemed meager (a phonograph in a salt-pitted cabinet, a recalcitrant-looking TV, the reading matter suggesting discards by passengers making luggage space for duty-free souvenirs), and everyone seemed pleased—except Ray, in the midst of what might be his most important story and not at all inclined to share it.

The Captain proposed they would later take a vote and give the winner a Christmas party on board when he cast anchor at York Island on Christmas Eve. "I discharge by lighter at York Town," (only half audible through the ladies' delighted buzz set off by "party"), adding like a mother-hostess to gathered-about children that they would draw straws for position, holding out a browned hand behind his head with, "The ballots, Erik?" which he tapped even at the exposed ends and offered all round like after-dinner cigars—pausing as he reached Ray to explain that Mr. Ray was a book publisher "and may hear something he can turn into a best seller" (cut short by "Mr. Ray's" quick protest that his house didn't publish fiction, and that in any case he was on a holiday).

Holiday?—Awake in his bunk for hours wondering how he could play along in the little game (he seemed to be sixth or seventh) and at the same time hold back the very story that was in the front of his mind, the story indeed of his being on the ship at all; wondering accompanied by the far-down mumbling in the engine room, by the hiss of warm air through his wide-open porthole, the sleepy rocking of the vessel that even when he put out the light continued to show the oscillating pale ghost of his white dinner jacket, on a hanger to save its being crushed by half a week in a suitcase and spoiling, marring anyway, his entrance—re-entrance—into the life of someone he hadn't seen in so long, the last time still wrapped in train sounds, night sounds, closing doors, her face pale in the narrowing crack of a door and gone, the sharp click of the latch saying "end" as distinctly as a voice, to which was added now the uncomfortable fact that she didn't know he was coming, that he deliberately hadn't told her, afraid she would say—write—"Don't you dare!"

And coming by water when a plane would have delivered him before a ship got well under way, explaining again to himself that he didn't want mere transportation, wanted a feeling of distance, of change in keeping with his change of outlook (possible change), wanted a sense of leaving, passing through, arriving some place else. He didn't want to look down on the Island with his head still full of the mainland, didn't want to go knocking at her door or ringing her telephone or seeing her face until he had considered everything again—re-considered, in the sense of maybe thinking better of the whole romantic plan, sentimental in a way he should have long outgrown. The years had rained down on her as well as him; they would have passed on the street without knowing each other.

Unless he heard her speak; he would know her voice, the tilt of her head if she laughed, the sort of thing that made her laugh. He loved her, but he also *liked* her, with the liking that underscores a love, the stem that carries the flower; he needed her, had felt a need of her at every clouded moment of a mostly sunny marriage, had often faced down the skeptic mocking him from a corner of himself: "The one that got away?" And now, three years after the accident, old but not old-old, hair a sable silvered (in Horatio's terms), he needed her in ways he hadn't known before, in ways the overheated young wouldn't understand, or value if they did. Not just another body but another presence, another consciousness—and not just "another" but hers.

Lonesome? No-and-yes. No, during the day; at the office with the others, a staff in more than one sense, his prop of questions and decisions (that he leaned on as he had the "walker" of his invalid months), his two or three current authors and their ingenious complaints. But afterhours was another matter, as if well-being faded with the sun. Lonesome then? Well, anyway, lonesome enough one night to half remember what the eagle said to Chaucer about *his* afterhours—something like, "Instead of reste and newe things, thou goest home to thy hous anoon, and also dumb as any stoon, thou sittest at another book, till fully dazed is thy look, and livest thus as an hermyte, althou thine abstinence is lyte."

At a bookshelf, in the midst of looking it up when Isabel phoned from Connecticut, she and Mary friends in college and the three of them in the New York years—widow now. "I'm going to Florida, Ted, to spend a week or so with

Sister. I could take a plane over from Atlanta for a day or two if that's convenient, for old time's sale." "Of course it's convenient." "If not, then on my way back?" "It's perfect."

Why not Isabel? Why did it have to be Claudia? Just wanting the remote instead of the near? the chancy instead of the possible, the possibly possible?—the white pendulum of his dinner jacket melting away into the clang of Erik's hand bell from the deck outside, *pianissimo*, to *forte* as he passed, to *pianissimo*, and the porthole full of horizontal, point-blank, booming-at-you sunlight.

And then, day after day, bearing almost straight down, reminding you the Equator was just over the horizon, he and the Doctor in deck chairs in the shade out of the sticky wind, the Doctor saying he "took a dislike to the boy—man—the minute he walked in my office." There watching the sky to the northeast light up in occasional bursts like a lantern uncovered then covered again, the back of his chair nudging his shoulders now and then as if this part of the Gulf Stream needed a resurfacing job.

"Tall, good-looking, twenty-five to thirty. Southerner. 'G-mawnin, Dr. Geltstein,' ('steen,' as they say down there). Confident. Not put-on Jew-confident. Goy-confident, the real article. All the things I wasn't, why shouldn't I dislike him?" with a short laugh at himself that was like moving to protect a chess piece he had carelessly pushed into a trap. "Two or three years in the Navy, resigned, married the girl-he-left-behind-him and brought her up to the University while he got his Ph.D in anthropology—hoped to get it. Confident he would. Tuckwell, Oscar Tuckwell. Her name was Meg, in Barbados now—"

Breaking off as the Captain passed on his afternoon prowl, white-top cap (once-white) on the back of his head pushing out his ears like pink ventilators, first mate at his heels with clipboard and pencil (Kristine-cat following along with monumental indifference). "Ya, a little weather, maybe," when Ray mentioned the lightning—"vetter," actually, pronunciation sometimes wanting but fluent in the language—moving on to pointing now and then at this and that, first mate jotting.

Not enough to turn the Doctor off his subject but it did, and Ray said, "Tuckwell?" after a minute to pull him back, sensing the possibility of something for his Press after all (the Company on its feet again following a season of all but disastrous success—a wish-fulfillment book called *Life Beyond the Grave*, which hit a sort of metaphysical jack pot and trapped the Press between pay-on-delivery printers of edition after edition and jobbers paying in ninety days, if then; the Press on pins and needles about ordering a new edition, vulnerable to having orders suddenly dry up with the books still at the bindery).

"Sewanee, Washington & Lee, some such place. Masters from Emory—a long story," dropping it as Preacher Bickle snapped their picture with the new camera he said his church had given him (his "5-church circuit") and sat down beside them.

"I spent twelve years with the circus before I found the Lord," as if dealing words off the top of his mind like cards off a worn deck already shuffled to suit him. "Drove the famous Forty-Horse Bandwagon through the streets of Paris for Barnum & Bailey. Frogs everywhere. Cheers. *Vivre! Toujours!* They had never seen the like. Took eight hours. Stopped now and then for ten minutes to rest my hands. Mayor of Paris gave me a medal. Lost it to the lion tamer in a poker game. I was a bad boy. Then I saw the light. Coming at me like the headlight on a steam engine . . . ."

They had been to the races, the Holiday Steeplechase (not the Preacher, who was done with "playing the ponies"), the Captain and Mrs. Captain, Geltstein and Ray—the Captain in double-breasted going-ashore brown, shiny in places, and white-top cap, Mrs. in something dark and Sundayish, years-ago Sundayish, had watched through the thick tropical glare as the lead horse in the third race stumbled, rolled, pitched off the black jockey in his Christmas-tree shirt, tried to get up, fell back, lay quivering in the powdery sand and in less than a minute had a bullet in his head from a pistol in the hand of a small man in a derby dressed in blue serge—everybody on his feet in the flimsy stands, Mrs. Captain turning her head, the Captain watching it all as he might watch a deck hand chipping paint, the Doctor tensed, one hand tight on the seat-back in front of him.

Mrs. Lundquist wanted to leave and Ray thought the Doctor did too but all of them stood there for a minute or two while a barefoot boy went scampering off toward the stables, danced round a skinny stable-hand already walking out behind a pair of mules hitched to a singletree dragging a chain and returned with him, eager to help with looping the chain about the horse's flat neck; she turned her head as the cortege got under way, the chain pulling up the long jawbone and stretching out the neck like old rubber with no elasticity left. They followed her out, picking their way between the half-filled benches, the Captain following last, stopping in an aisle to see the rest of it, reluctant to go until everything was shipshape again.

All of it wiped out of Ray's mind by the churn of life in the Square, the din of motor horns and motors, the imperturbable thereness of the blue-black cop at the crossing, solid on his thick-soled shoes, three-inch red slash down the seam of his black pants, white jacket, leather belt, white British helmet; by his signaling to a rattletrap car from the hills with an elegant forearm and wrist to his shoulder: everything shipshape in the Square.

"Don't shove off without us," shouting through the racket as they separated.

"Na-a!" with his Norwegian laugh. "I vistle," pulling twice on a make-believe cord by the rim of his cap, gold dental work shining (the Preacher in a doorway catching all of it with an inaudible click and a country smile).

And he and Geltstein had frosted pineapple drinks in the garden of the hotel and talked a little about themselves, not much—the Doctor going to Barbados to give three lectures at the College, "Codrington, know some people with a place near Bridgetown" (the words later popping into Ray's mind at the Doctor's, "Her name was Meg, in Barbados now"); Ray mentioning San Juan de Pinos and saying he had a friend there (wondering if he really did). Both of them clearly more at ease on their shipmates: Pyt who said he was a diver, a thin man with an old sunburn and a reddish beard getting gray in places (passing round a gold coin he said was a Spanish doubloon, "Minted in Colon, 1621. Off the *San Fernando*"), Frank Hardly and his wife from Colorado who had never seen the sea and thought a boat ride to Surinam and back would be a nice way to spend the Holidays ("Gave the boys at the plant two weeks, I manufacture pickles, store the cukes a year in brine, Colorado's famed for cukes, the Japs grow the best ones''), Preacher Bickle with his camera (''Gift from my flock, boat ticket too, they love me, God bless 'em'), the two young woman from Alabama going to Paramaribo where the husband of one of them was in the Consulate (''Romance is my hobby,'' Geltstein quoting the younger as saying with a bright laugh).

And going on after a silence, ''Years ago a chap came up to Princeton to work with a colleague of mine for a Ph.D. in anthropology,'' Ray thinking later it was the mention of the Southern women that put him in mind of the Southerner who was ''Goy-confident, the real article,'' though still later he wondered if it wasn't the business at the racetrack that reminded him, the pistol-shot in the sunny afternoon; stopping as if sorry he had begun and pointing off at the top-heavy palms and the buzzards high up in the sky like the cookbooks' ''freshly-ground pepper,'' circling idly as though waiting for bedtime to tumble into the hotel trees. ''Friends of mine at Emory wrote me he was coming, top-grade student and—'' the deep ''vistle'' rolling in over the palms like a gust of wind that might have shaken them, lifting both to their feet, the Doctor downing the last of his drink, Ray leaving the rest of his.

They overtook the two women on the dock, halfway out among the pink stacks of pine, barrels of salt fish, cylinders of oxygen, bags of maize, crates stenciled *Quinine Tonic* (with a tropical overtone), all of it under a squeaky spicy rosin smell mixed with ocean smell. They were talking to a bearded white man in a ragged straw hat and torn-off shirt sleeves who seemed to be asking for money and looked as if he could use it. One of the women was opening a hand purse when a man who might have been the head stevedore—khaki jacket, swagger stick in his armpit, sharp black features like a white actor in a minstrel show—approached them at an easy stroll and the beggar hopped away.

''Save your money, ladies,'' cigarette moving in the middle of his front teeth. ''I chase him off every time a ship ties up with American dollars.'' As they passed Ray heard, ''. . . on the beach. . . got in trouble, lost his papers. . . Q-mum,'' pocketing what would have bought another drink for the wino—making Publisher Ray wish he had time to overtake him and maybe get a book for his *Sunwise Press* (even if Conrad and Stevenson had already written it).

Geltstein said, ''All aboard, ladies,'' and a few steps on, the ladies passed them, running on ahead and up the gangplank—in jeans this time. Skirts the morning they joined the cruise in Tampa, joined the four passengers in one of the ships boats, the vessel alongside the wharf but taking on the travelers from the harbor side because of the shifting engines, the cranes and winches and cables swinging the blond lumber. ''Not much more, folks!'' from the first mate, shouted through the clatter with a sympathetic grin from where he stood on a thwart to hold the boat against the ten-foot vertical ladder lashed to the dock while one of them (who became Frank Hardly from Greeley, Colorado) gallantly climbed part way up to assist the ladies—specifically to help them hold down their skirts against the Gulf wind; which he managed very well with the first one, standing close against her and guiding her down almost in his arms. The other one, impatient at waiting, took to the ladder on her own, pulling her skirt between her legs and trying to hold it there but needing both hands for the ladder and the skirt whipping free against her elbows; glancing round the boat with a pink-and-white laugh when she was down and, "Sorry!", dismissing it with, "I'm Mrs. Ackworth, everybody. Sarah-Wesley. And this is my cousin Rebecca, Miss Newberry." Miss Newberry gaily exclaiming, "Oh, 'Becky,' please!" (Mrs. Hardly's broad fingers still against her blushes at the flash of white underpants), the mate pushing off and rowing under the salt-eaten crag of the bow—

"Ready, Mr. Edward Ray of the *Sunwise Press*?" as if exulting at snapping handcuffs on a fugitive, handing him the newspaper folded back to show "Arrivals & Departures" at the bottom of the front page and what looked like (without his glasses) "Book Publisher among those arriving today by the *Lindvagen*" and a little more he couldn't read, she all spic and span in cotton skirt and blouse and bright silk handkerchief at her chin, leaning a forearm on the high back of another chair and watching him as if half expecting him to deny it, he for a moment thinking less about her seeing the lines than about the possibility (probability?) of Claudia seeing them too, trying to reassure himself that Claudia wouldn't be studying "Arrivals & Departures" as this woman had been—and no doubt her husband too—drawn to it by wondering about this visitor they had rescued; and then telling himself "Book Publisher" wouldn't give him away to Claudia (he hadn't been in that end of book publishing in those days), then completely reassured at remembering Claudia wouldn't have seen the paper, wasn't on the Island, was "expected by lunchtime tomorrow, sir, is there a message?"

Thanking her again for their rescue of him (almost repeating his "Apollo appears from above with Helen"—still pleased with it), she interrupting him with, "Come on. Peter's all but ready—there he is" (at a beep from below). "Oh, bathroom! Inside, first door on your right, don't see the mess, we'll be in the car."

Five minutes in a confusion of damp towels, a dangling bra, dripping tan stockings on a shower door that reminded him of marriage like a wedding ring, and they were off with the masculine "vroom" usually promoted by alcohol or female passenger. Not much talk, with the wind and the speed and the air of semi-Britishness about them; once an offhand, "Tyner—Janet, Peter" with a move of his thumb on the wheel. No further mention of "Edward Ray," as if everyone understood names hardly mattered with their association ending in a few minutes at the steps of his hotel. Once, halfway in, he caught himself about to ask if they knew a Mrs. Martha Freeland who had recently taken a house on the Island; they well might know her, well might know her visiting mother Claudia, well might pass on news about this stranded Mr. Ray they had picked up, make it too late to change his mind, "re-consider," take flight—not flying well but somehow always in flight—the thought as if creating the airport in front of them, not his hotel, planes hovering like doves over a baited field, Peter maneuvering into a spot of shade and pulling the handbrake with a metallic chirp. "Jan will take you in in just a minute, do you mind?"

Ray said, "Take your time," getting out now to give her room to pass, she sliding across and out and leaving behind her as the two of them went arm-in-arm into the terminal the faint presence of a scent that he recognized but couldn't remember what flower it came from, as a face can puzzle you when you can't supply the name, now suddenly lifted back as if on a rainbow of scents to a long-ago moment of becoming conscious of the scent that Claudia wore, not jasmin, maybe not perfume at all but soap from washing her black hair, good soap, costly—beside him in the car singing nursery songs in Canadian French (from school days in Quebec) as they drove in the summer mountains, Mary and Mot in the back, the scent there and not there like early mist thin on the slopes blowing in and out; breaking off her song with "Look at that!" as they crossed a bridge over a dizzy white waterfall, leaving the car on a shoulder and the four of them walking back to look down into the gorge. Missing Mot, "Where's Mot?" and catching sight of him climbing the guard rail.

"Mot, what are you doing!" from Mary.

No answer, Mot hopping from rock to rock and sitting down on the brink staring into the well of churning-up steam. "What's the matter with you! Come back up here!"

And quietly from Claudia, "Leave him alone. He's annoyed."

All of it drifting inch by inch, moment by moment, into the other gorge, chasm, abyss, unacknowledged but noted by some of the canny fledgling senses, his certainly and possibly hers.

"Mot has to go to Asheville in the morning," one afternoon, August, the summer all but gone.

"You are going too?

"Spend the day in Asheville? Mercy on us!" Creating a day between them, Elysian, halcyon, beatific, if he hadn't been afraid of deflating it with a word—wading in a swift river at a spot she knew, skirt in her forearms, white legs turning pink in the mountain water, the pink making colored stockings to where it ended; a movement at a corner of his eye and a pale thread looping out beyond a bend as a fisherman in glistening boots followed his casts upstream, so intent on picking his target, aiming, casting his line they escaped to the bank unseen, escaped to a grass-covered shelf on the bank and lay motionless while he passed beyond the overhanging limbs, beyond their laughs smothered in each other's hands, each other's mouths. Then, "I love you, Eddie. What are we going to do?" (Do?—He loved two women, level on his balances, as an ounce of civet balanced an ounce of musk. Choose one over the other? morning over afternoon? April over May? And then watching those questions changing like clouds before a wind, changing their brightness into, for him, disquieting shapes and shadows: the ambiguity of her knowing the spot already—the seclusion, the shelf—germinating in his mind, and one season, months away, in its own good time, pushing a soft green shoot of distrust up through his beatitude.)

Then, fumbling in her handbag for her ticket to Charleston in a Penn Station full of a dozing rumble, ten minutes to midnight and train time on the dangling moon-clock, passengers on the way to muffled green-draped Pullman tunnels, tables on the Roman floor for navy-blue officials, envelopes, pencils, ticket punches, pale yellow diagrams for berths taken and free.

"You don't have to wait, Edward," (to the handbag—to "Edward," not "Eddie"), rather stiff. As she had been all evening: all week, or on the two times she had allowed herself to be seen. Alone in New York, the two of them, he to wind up loose ends after moving to Georgia, she on some errands of her own that he had taken as pretext for being with him. And then excuses: "Not tonight, Peggy's planning something" (whoever "Peggy" was—she seemed to be staying with "Peggy"), and "shopping with Peggy," and "to the doctor with Peggy," and he finally said, "All right, we'll go out to dinner and take 'Peggy'." "Oh, thank you, we couldn't do that,"—even the "thank you" distant.

And now, folded green ticket in her fingers, "Don't wait, Edward. Please. I'd rather you didn't."

"You've been avoiding me."

"What do you mean, Edward?"

"Why?"

"Why what?"

"Why avoiding me?" Seeming not to hear him, smiling at the conductor as she handed over her ticket as though to say she could smile if she cared to.

"But why?" from him as they waited, her eyes on the conductor's pale indoor hands tearing, marking, stamping. "But why?" when she showed no sign of hearing him, smiling again at receiving back what was left of the ticket, putting it away, glancing at her porter.

She moved off from the table, fingering for something in the handbag (or for nothing) than, halting, lifted her head and closed the bag with a snap that somehow carried over into her voice. "It's got to be more or less, Edward," words level, eyes level, straight into his.

"And you are saying you want it less?"

"You don't want it more.—Go on now. Good-by." Then, "What are you doing?" as he laid on the table his ticket to Baltimore.

"I'm on this train too," her face becoming a complexity of dark anger like a sudden squall at the surprise of it, at the trick (who had tried to trick?—one of the long-lived questions), apprehension, uncertainty. "You're *what*!" He said he had to go to Baltimore, had an appointment with a doctor in the morning.

She seemed to hold herself still for the purpose of drawing a breath deep into her chest then slowly expelling it with, "You don't look very sick," more suspicious than concerned, but with a glimmer of concern.

"Routine. A man named Goodwin. I've seen him before," handing a porter the check for his suitcase and some money and pointing at the checkroom.

"And you don't act sick either," voice stinging, eyes almost laughing.

"Routine."

She studied him for long enough to be counting slowly up to five, then ten, the dozing hum of the station soft-falling like early snow, then said, "You win," put her arm through his and they went down the iron stairs to the black train in step, to the compartment he had slyly taken ("drawing room" in those days).

Not yet daybreak in Baltimore, a shadow-streaked sharp October morning, the warmth of her arms still against his cheeks and ears, of her waist and back against his hands, the smooth hard-soft guitar-frets of her spine, of her guarded, pale, withdrawing face in the slice of the door closing as if the gripping brakes were closing it, features solemn to sad, then "End" as distinctly as a voice, quietly stated it—and never a word from her or sight of her for thirty years. Even after the accident, not a word (though, far away, she might never have heard of it; and so much time had come and gone).

But Isabel heard; phoned from Connecticut. And later phoned again: she could stop off for a day or two on her way to Florida if that was convenient. "Of course it's convenient, it's perfect." (And adequate for his story when his turn came round? Told him by "a friend"?—imitating the Doctor's "colleague of mine," probably also a red herring. Or by "one of our authors"?)

And there on the level deck with some of the others: "One of our authors, a man named Howard. About my age. Came to a fork in the road. Which way?", the sea oily and smooth and warm and the bow steady against the bottom of the sky, the dream of the stormy days come true, and leaving you without a dream.

THE "AUTHOR'S" TALE

They watched her plane, Howard and his daughter, holding ears against the scream of it creeping up on the man with the beckoning torches like a scolded dog. "Perfect," he had told her when she mentioned stopping off, but now confronting it, the pleasure of seeing her after so long became a dread of seeing what the years had done to her, of seeing that reflect what they had done to him—years that had crept up on him as gently as the plane, misreading his signals which meant, Stay where you are.

The plane then so suddenly silent it seemed to roll backward. And the years rolled backward too, with her easy descent of the landing stairs, not lightfooted—carefully, indeed—but coming down easily, hand on a rail but keeping her place with the others, cheeks and eyes in tissue-paper smile-wrinkles at seeing them, at being there, kissing them lightly, Howard then Emily, nothing in her face of funerals, cemeteries, condolences—ignoring, or not noticing, his still unmended leg.

And everything easy among the three of them back at home, as if the years had been too much occupied with changing surfaces to bother with the realities underneath; most of the changes in Emily anyway, changing kindergarten and Gracie Square for editor's desk and Madison Avenue. "Emily has to go back Monday morning, are you afraid to be alone in the house with me?"

She laughed, "Not in the least," and he

almost said, You were once, but changed it to, "I won't molest you."

"Howard!—I'll be leaving Thursday."

And Emily gone, easy between the two of them, comfortable in a loosely tied attraction, age-loosened, age-opulent. Open about herself as if speaking of someone else: children all married now, the youngest two months ago; she was selling her house, too much to keep up for one person, to heat, long hard Connecticut winters.

"Moving to Florida with your sister?"

"I love my sister, Howard, but I don't like Florida, and I can't stand my brother-in-law." No, she had a friend who was delighted with a new project in Virginia, "apartments in a country setting for 'retired people,' a nice way of saying 'Old Folks'." She had stopped off on her way down to see her. "And *it.* Some drawbacks of course. But I'm not going to live with one of my children. Or trek about the country from one to another."

Howard thinking what a reciprocal problem it was to his own. And wondering if that had occurred to her when she said, "You're keeping this house, Howard?" (or, indeed, if she had thought of it when she proposed stopping off on her way). He said he didn't know, hadn't decided, said the real-estate agents were on his trail, he believed they watched the funeral notices keeping tabs on widows and widowers.

Easy filling-in-the-years talk—handfuls of pebbles to fill the Grand Canyon—easy silences, not much host-and-guest in it. Ora Mae serving them lunch at the usual two o'clock after his usual morning at the Typewriter (capital T), setting her place as a matter of course at Mary's chair, not Emily's—he thought of correcting it but let it stand, it didn't matter, so short a visit. No strain between them he could feel.

Even easy talk-and-silence over the steak she broiled one night, she apparently making no connection with the other talk-and-silence over the other steak, he connecting but wary of the interpretation she might put on his reminding her and saying nothing: Mary in Kentucky on a visit home and he rattling round in New York emptiness for five days then calling her number. "Are you free for a movie or something, I'm going crazy." Come over about eight, she would do him a steak with mushrooms and mashed potatoes. And before he knew it, dishes in the sink, he was on his knees in front of her chair leaning into her lap with his arms round her waist. "You'd better go home now." "What do you mean? I'm not ready to go home." "Get your hat." "But I've just finished dinner, Isabel. It wouldn't be polite. My mother always said—" "Whatever your mother said, you're going home," and standing up. "But, Isabel—" "no 'buts,'" kissing him firmly on the mouth and pushing him out. Pushing him in effect to the phone and a train next morning for Kentucky.—And this night, dishes in the sink, kissing lightly and closing her door at one end of the January-humming house and he closing his at the other.

Tuesday evening in the living room, in Mary's chair but with the lamp tilted at an Isabel angle, closing a book on her finger in a temporary way, "You see, Howard, there's something good to be said for not succeeding with your books as you'd have liked to. Success is not the same as happiness, though sometimes from a distance—"

"You mean the art of losing isn't hard to master?"

"I didn't say that."

"A considerable poet did."

"I wouldn't say it wasn't hard, Howard, but it has its good points."

"Perhaps you would kindly name one?"

"Why, you'd be out of work now, frozen in a reputation. Afraid to write anything, afraid of breaking something."

He said the only good point in it he could see was you could lift out something you liked from one book and use it again in book after book and nobody complained or knew the difference. "I've done that."

"I know you have. I didn't complain because I was glad to see it again," smiling a moment then brushing it aside with, "God damn it, Howard, you always try to turn it off with a laugh!" pulling out her finger and going on with her reading—*Catherine the Great,* he remembered because he had said Mary had a copy and she said, "This is it. I found it in the bedroom. Bookmark in Chapter One," holding it up, "a tape from the supermarket."

"She hated supermarkets, one and all. Hated housekeeping."

"Who doesn't?"

"Once she wrote PLEASE, ORA MAE! with her finger in the coating of dust on a bedroom mirror. I don't know how long it stayed there—why do you laugh?"

"It's still there. Or was. I fixed it." (As much as saying—what? That mirrors weren't dusty in her house? That his mirrors wouldn't be dusty if she had charge of them?)

Telling her on Thursday as she was closing her suitcase he wanted her to have something of Mary's and handing her Mary's gold wristwatch. "No, I won't take that. But I'll take the book.—And the bookmark."

Ora Mae said, "Nice lady," serving him lunch at the empty table, and he said, Yes she was, school friend of Miss Mary's (using the old-style 'Miss-Mary" business because that was the language he was brought up on, and Ora Mae too).

"So she said."

"You-all had a visit?"

Oh yes, she drove to "the store" with her two or three times. "Wanted to know how you were getting on. I said you miss Miss Mary, we all did. She said you need somebody. I said, why don't you marry Mr. Howard, Miss Isabel?"

"You didn't!" knocking grains of rice on to the tablemat as from a clap of thunder. And after a gulp, two gulps, recovering the rice grain by grain, "What did she say to that?

"She said she suppose nobody could take Miss Mary's place."

"I see. Well, you-all certainly did have 'a visit'!"

And asking himself, Why not? It sounded like a rather halfhearted No; and reading the other ambiguities of her visit as they might be read (including the visit itself), might be hardly a No at all. Offering a solution for both of them that was like finding the key word to the puzzle? No more agents trying to sell his house from under him; no more seeking out homes for 'Old Folks" in Virginia—or in Georgia. Everything would drop into place, the telephone drawing his eye as if it had rung.

Suppose he called her; not to settle such a momentous matter over the phone but, say, to ask her to have lunch with him in Atlanta on her way home? Yes, he liked that. . . .

He couldn't phone her! He didn't know her sister's name, didn't know the name of anyone who might know it. The children all with married names he didn't know—

Ray turning out his hands in finality, and stirring up an indignant chorus of: "He let her get away!" "Made for each other!" "Dumb cluck!" "She gave him every chance!" "Men!"

Becky said, "The bastard shouldn't have let her come down if he wasn't going to stuff her."

"Please, Cousin!"

"No need to insult her."

Ray said he believed the man was still grieving over the death of his wife, and Mrs. Hardly came to his support with, "Of course he was. A Japanese gentleman on the farm next to us—Mr. Yamamoto, Frank, (raised beautiful cucumbers)—he said when his wife died he died too. He needed a wife to help him with the cukes—"

"Help him with the cukes!"

"—but women didn't look like women to him any more, if you follow me." (Cousin

Becky laughing that she followed her.) "He went to a Japanese doctor in Denver—"

"You mean it wouldn't stand up?"

Mrs. Hardly answering only by fanning away a non-existent Colorado gnat and rolling up her eyes to the overhead racks of life preservers.

And Ray alone in the midst of them, alone with himself and 'Howard' (and "Mr. Yamamoto") in the January house with the furnace humming much the same tune as rose up now from the engine room, alone and sleepy, without the faintest desire to go back down the hall and tap on her closed door—beyond it the woman he had once knelt in front of, leaning into her lap with his arms round her body; who might not send him away this time. What was the matter with him?

And not the first time he had asked the question. Showing a young real estate agent about the house when he was considering whether or not to list it, move to smaller quarters. A slim bareheaded girl dressed in a two-piece something that he thought showed a nice awareness of what was fitting for both office desk and living room, pad and pencil in and out of a shoulder bag for notes on this and that, opening closets, looking in and about, in no hurry—starting the dish washer, listening to the air conditioner, lighting the oven, lighting all burners on top of the stove. "Two bathrooms?" flushing both toilets. "Built-in shower? Yes," opening the glass door that had often closed on Mary and him in the laughing days; wanting to see the attic and climbing the steep stairs indifferent to much tan stockings and garter clips showing, but no more than he was. And indifferent beside her as she felt the mattress of the double bed, not wondering how she would be with her hair spread out on the pillow and her shoes kicked off but how soon he could wind up her visit and get rid of her; not wondering if he would ask her out to dinner to finish up their questions and answers, just wondering how soon she would go.—What was the matter with him?

It was as if the accident had been a lightning flash that left him in a dark house pushing dead switches, stumbling about for candles; and settling after a time for quiet old lamps with wicks and kerosene and before long telling himself the softer light and shadows were rather pleasing; or as if he had moved into a cabin in the woods with everything at hand but electricity, quiet forest voices he had forgotten, deep many-leveled silences. Call in an electrician? Why? He could see things that were obscured before.

And yet: "Testosterone," white jacket, eyes drawing a bead on him over half-glasses, as sure-footed as a service man reaching up to close the master panel of circuit breakers. "Very simple. Ten minutes. Stop in once a week, any of the nurses can handle it if I am tied up. A simple shot in the hip." "Every week!" "Or you might consider the longer-lasting procedure. An analeptic injection of slow-release tablets into the lower abdomen. No pain, no discomfort. I have patients who come in twice a year . . . ." (like lighting your house from a tank of propane gas in the yard that you refilled from time to time).

No thank you. Eyes getting used to the dark; that was really more of a light-change than a dimness, revealing as much as it obscured, revealing meadow land and easy-winding roads in place of switchbacks skirting mountain canyons, deadly drop-offs. Revealed his need for today's Claudia—or the Claudia she might be if she was as glad to leave the area of zig-zag emotions as he was—

Revealing the young woman's gawky flat-foot woman-trot as she hurried across the parking area, reminding him of the agent as she finally trotted off to her car, the same age and shape ("One in girth, in coif, in cadence, Lithe and blithe of limb and look," sisters in his new-found liberation); and this one thankfully soon to drop him off at the steps of his hotel with, no doubt, a gay flutter of young wrist like a rising pigeon.

"Sorry you had to wait,—Mr. Edward Ray of the *Sunwise Press*," folding herself under the wheel as neatly as running a comb through her hair, using his name as if she enjoyed shining a light on him from her obscurity, he mumbling something about not being in a hurry, plenty of things to worry about if you were in his business, and she starting the motor with the offhandedness of a mother scooping up a child. "Poor Peter. They keep him on the run. Continental Drug. Medical supplies among the islands." Waiting at a light she said, "Can I take you somewhere? Are you familiar with our Island?"

He said he was familiar with the bus service, which made her laugh as she had laughed at *"Helen,"* a short surprised laugh that flicked a color on and off her jawbone. She said, "Yes," and after a pause, "You shouldn't have taken the bus."

"I see that now."

"They're touchy. We're all touchy. Touchy as half-brothers and-sisters, Jerry says. Step-parents all divorced or dead or both. He says something's burning but we don't know where . . . ." breaking off as the light went green. He almost said, "'Jerry?'"not because he cared but as you let the young talk about what interests them or there won't be any talk, and no matter anyhow; two or three more lights and she would have "vroomed" away.

The thought bringing back a childish instant in a swimming pool foreseeing the withdrawal of a hand from under his chin; could he stay afloat through a solitary afternoon and evening in a strange island he had no interest in until a distant "lunchtime tomorrow"? But if, instead of merely thanking her at the hotel steps, he asked her in for a drink he could certainly expect a transparent excuse coated with a film of youth-to-age; and if she came in, sat a while on the broad porch, the result would be worse, so far apart in years their voices would hardly carry, assuredly wouldn't carry the overtones they started with, references, opinions, standards, beliefs all lost in the valleys. Contemporary with the two young women on the ship but different in a way as hard to define as the differences, for Western eyes, in the faces of Orientals; all three with layers of individuality like undercurrents in a stream but a suggestion in this one of levels, or just a level, under the others, the stream not quite so clear, maybe no deeper but the depth obscured, indeterminate. For him. Hazy as a page of manuscript without his glasses—that really did't appeal to him enough to make him put them on.

He said, "How do you like living on an island?" (just to bring up something to interest her—a little sorry that it came out suggesting a ball tossed underhand for a child to catch).

She skipped answering in a way she seemed to have of going on as if she *had* answered. "Jerry once sent us out to cover one of their get-togethers in the back country. 'Cain and Abel,' it seemed to me. No words I understood, but I could follow. No pictures though. They took the camera. Gave it back."

He said, "Cain and Abel?" watching for the white front of the *Princess Ann.*

"Gran Met, they say, is the Creator of heaven and earth but the Almighty Master created the Universe. He's too busy to bother with daily problems down here, has delegated spirits to help him—Loa. They say a man searching for a lost horse saw a flash of light in a palm grove and looking up saw a Loa nestled in the palms pointing into the woods. He crossed himself and called to her to thank her and she flew away in the shape of a pigeon—Here we are."

"Will you come in?" still expecting an excuse—and rather hoping—the invitation escaping like the Loa, she accepting without a word in a movement of locking the ignition and opening her door.

She might have been the one to invite him, more at home in the hotel than he was, speaking to 'Thomas" who took their order and brought it out to porch chairs with wide flat arms like schoolroom chairs but cushioned and with slanted backs suggestive of heat and loose clothes and easy-does-it. She waved at a crooked little sign across the street (that he was glad to realize he could read at this distance): "'*22 Taxis Facing West*.' Usually two, sometimes one," pausing for a moment then going on with what he came to think was really on her mind. "Peter wanted to drop you off on the way in and save you a wait at the airport. I said, No. But you'd never guess why."

He said he hadn't minded waiting.

"You wouldn't guess I was a writer, would you?"

He was mean enough to say it was never safe to assume a lady wasn't, laughing a little not to hurt her feelings but seeing ahead of him the probability of having to read something and contrive a kindly negative; he had faced other over-the-transoms but none that landed more unexpectedly than the one he could foresee.

She had written some poetry that "Jerry" had printed in the *Islander* when she was on the paper. "Second grade, I'm sure. Or third. Anyway, no pay. Somebody said only a blockhead would write without pay, but I think only a blockhead would say such a thing.'' He mumbled something about ''Dr. Johnson,'' but it didn't divert her. She said she had a half-done novel that was better than the poetry. ''Maybe no good, but—yes, good,'' he trying to arrange an escape by saying his company didn't publish fiction, and much relieved at the reappearance of their waiter and her making an expert leap to, ''Thomas, is Mr. Hugh Jim here today?''

Thomas, wary as his Georgia cousins, said he couldn't say about that, and she, understanding the idiom as well as Ray did, said to tell him she would like to speak to him, turning then to Ray and saying perhaps he would like to see something of the back country. ''Maybe worth the trip, maybe not. Rites? Rituals? Maybe nothing. You never know. Or is your evening spoken for?'' Confronting him with an immediate decision: off with this subtly foreign, pushy young woman to tourist ''sights'' he was too old to have room for, or off to bed with a paperback under a slow-turning ceiling fan possibly not turning at all after a ten-o'clock curfew.

'''Adam and Eve,' once, somebody told us. Not Christians, where did they get it? And maybe it wasn't 'Adam and Eve' at all . . . . Hugh Jim,'' to a tall black man in a chef's pleated toque that made him seem all but majestic, ''Mr. Ray is a distinguished visitor to San Juan de Pinos. He would like to see something of the real island, the mountains, the Cockpit country, the people—the sort of thing you once arranged for Mr. Jerry on the paper; remember?'' Hugh Jim gazing down slantways as if at something between him and the broad cypress planks of the floor. When he said nothing she said, ''Remember?'' again and he waited a minute as if for a sauce to settle then shook his head. ''Not the right season, madam.''

Surprised, she asked, Why not? and he said, ''Christmas-time, madam. Old year dying, new year borning—''

''Yes, but—''

''New day borning—''

''Well, all right, but—''

''Not a time for visitors,'' moving from one glistening shoe to the other, obviously anxious to be gone.

She persisted with, ''You could arrange it, Hugh Jim,'' giving Ray the idea she wanted to go for reasons of her own, probably for filling out something in her book (already a member of the ruthless-author clan).

"On duty tonight, madam," finality in the shake of the white cap, she dismissing him with a petulant wave then calling him back and handing him ten dollars with, "Christmas gift, Hugh Jim."

Taking him back for an instant—street lights coming on—to the Christmas lanterns strung about the deck of the anchored ship and Sarah-Wesley talking to the mate, talking down a little, eyes on the others dancing to the phonograph. "Take a drink, Mr. First Mate. You're not having any fun," the mate smiling at his cup of punch, taking an obedient sip and as the music ended going to the turntable and changing the record, she beside him, shoulders rocking on the memory of the old tune and, as the new one started, opening her arms to be danced with—

Janet saying, "Never mind, there are other ways," in much the manner of Sarah-Wesley concerned that the mate was "not having any fun,'' standing up with, ''I'll ask Jerry,'' and leaving Ray to phone him from the lobby—leaving him dancing with Cousin Becky but thinking of the other two, Sarah-Wesley feather-light on her debutante feet, the mate's big shoes threatening a collision at each step and she by some laser-beam signal to her toes moving them in the nick of time, the mate not able to see it but conscious of it and smiling at her spread of white teeth. Bits of their talk drifting to him laced into the music: ''You really think I'm lightheaded, don't you?'' ''Lightheaded? What is lightheaded? I think you are beautiful-headed.'' A turn of the record, two or three turns, then, ''Well, you know you're rather handsome yourself, Mr. Mate.''

And little laughs back and forth, the music ending and the mate changing the record and filling two cups from the bowl, she dancing by herself while she waited, lifting a cup from him as she passed then holding out her arms, teasing him with, ''They must teach dancing at your Navigation School.''

''No time for dancing.''

''But you are a beautiful dancer,'' pushing back at his shoulder when he held her closer, lowering her eyes, offended but forgiving, falling back on some country-club chatter ("How often do you make this trip, Mr. Wagman?"— "Mr. Wagman" itself a slight push at his shoulder—and, "I suppose you are never seasick, Mr. Mate?"), which he ignored: "Would you like to see my School? I have pictures." "Oh, yes I would." "Come, I'll show you." "My cousin would like to see them too. Becky!" But Becky was listening to the Doctor. "Wait a minute for Becky." "You change your mind, you do not want to see them." "Oh, but I do—"

"He's not in the office. But he's expected. I'll go talk to him, it isn't far. Thomas, bring Mr. Ray something to wait with. Ten minutes, Edward, no more. Maybe twelve." And off down the steps at a sure-footed run that brought back the sure-footed real estate woman, the two of them merging for an instant, both young, both persistent with purposes involving him—list a house, read a manuscript (not quite proposed yet but casting its shadow)—and he with an instinctive negative for each; that in the case of this one grew weaker as he waited: suppose her book was built somehow on "Gran Met"and "Almighty Master" and "Loas", as her interest in all that suggested, wasn't that reaching into the same metaphysical area as the Press's best seller of a few years ago? If she had told it simply, with enough first-hand freshness, mightn't it be edited into another *Beyond the Grave?* (Fiction, she called it, but there was usually less fiction in fiction than the author believed.)

"Beyond the Grave" taking him back to the ship and the funeral service for the Captain's aunt, the Captain reading through his wire-rimmed spectacles at the leeward end of the bridge, his passengers at the rail below, the thin pages of the Prayer Book fluttering in the light wind like captured birds: *"Unto Almighty God we commend the soul of our sister departed,"* through his bull-horn, the ship hardly making steerageway, the sky hardly light enough to let him read but getting brighter every second as the sun pushed up, all of them at a seemly remove from the mate with the urn containing the ashes—inviting them all at dinner to the sunrise service, explaining that the old lady had asked to be buried at sea with her forebears but the authorities would not release the body except in the form of ashes after cremation. *"And we commit her body to the deep,"* signaling and pausing while the mate dipped into the urn with a wooden spoon from the galley and cast a spoonful of ashes south and west. *"In sure and certain hope of the Resurrection"* (signaling again) *"unto eternal life, through our Lord Jesus Christ,"* signaling again, and the mate casting another spoonful.

And while the Captain waited, watching over his glasses, another. And then another, the Captain continuing, holding down the restless pages, the new sun horizontal against his cheek, *"At whose coming in glorious majesty to judge the world"* (signaling) *"the sea shall give up her dead, and the corruptible bodies of those who sleep in her"* (signaling again) *"shall be changed,"* pulling off his reading glasses to focus the mate better and motioning with some impatience to get on with it. *"And made like unto his glorious body, according to the mighty working whereby* . . . how much more you got?"

The mate making a sort of helpless gesture

indicating the situation was beyond his control, and the Captain shouting, "Dump it! ...*whereby he is able to subdue all things unto himself.*—Amen!"

And "Amen!" from the Reverend Marion Bickle, his arrival now at the end of the service suggesting a lingering annoyance at the Captain's having declined his offer to "assist." He made several quick shots of the group at the rail and the mate with the upturned urn, though the light was still hardly strong enough; and several shots, a few minutes later, of the passengers at early coffee served on a starboard deck out of the wind, spoons and saucers resuming a comfortable tinkle as if included in the Captain's orders to his engine room.

Ray had gingerly added a few drops of condensed milk to his coffee and was reaching for sugar when the diver, Pyt, pointed off to the southeast at what for a moment seemed empty sun-streaked water than showed a fleck of white that brought them all to the rail, Preacher Bickle first, staring at the spot then raising both arms in a Praise-the-Lord gesture and mumbling incoherent Bible words that might have been "taketh" and "giveth"—the

Captain evidently already aware of the object through his glass and ordering a change of course to bring it nearer.

Then there below them four blistered men in a weathered rowboat with a ragged makeshift sail that they loosened while they rocked on the quiet sea and shouted up for "Vater!—*De l'eau!—Wasser!"* and Preacher Bickle staring at the sky and mumbling something about "the quick and the dead."

The Captain said, "Throw him a line!" and a snake's-tongue line looped out from below into the four of them, then, "Come aboard?" through his horn in a questioning tone but as if knowing the answer, which was two or three parched shouts of "Vater! Vater!"

"Where you from?" in a comradely voice that was almost playful, gesturing an order to the mate to round up some supplies. Repeating, "Where you from?" after a minute but as though not surprised at needing to ask again, and drawing out a mumble among the boatmen and headshakes and a *"Comprends pas!"*

"You *'comprends'* plenty, I think."

"Vater! Vater!"

Ray and the rest watching while Erik and a deck hand lowered a demijohn of water and a basket of biscuits and cans, the rowboat rising and falling on the swell, sun-blackened arms reaching, guiding, the Captain shouting, "How's everything on the Island?" in a sociable tone.

"Comprends pas! 'Eye-land?' *Ques que c'est,* 'eye-land'?" but with a grin of broken teeth.

"Isle du Diable, n'est c'pas?"

Silence for a moment in the boat, then grumbles back and forth, then *"Merci, mon capitan. Bon voyage!"* freeing the line and shoving off with a hard push of an oar—for Preacher Bickle, shoving off among the resurrected ashes: "He counseleth the deep to receive our sister and resurrecteth three in her stead," on his knees at the rail, the camera swinging loose as if weighted with doctrine.

Geltstein murmuring, "Four, Deacon," and Bickle saying, "Were there four? My eyes are not what they were," the coffee spoons taking up their tinkle, the deck its micro-tremble from the engine room, the ensign on the stern lifting out behind them.

And reminding Ray of the Navy and the young lieutenant. "Tuckwell," he said; "did he get his Ph.D.? Confident he would,'goy-confident,' you remember,'' and the Doctor, gazing out over the stern as if at a sea of rolling years, went on with the rest of it—accounting, incidentally, for his presence on the ship (and, without meaning to, Ray's also, as the ship became more and more a House of Mirrors reflecting himself at every turn, misshapen, grotesque, distorted beyond recognition—almost).

THE DOCTOR'S COLLEAGUE'S TALE

My colleague—I'll call him ''X'', Dr. X, you'd probably know him, high up in his field (*the* field, you might say, ''digs'' and all that)—he had his handsome wife Donna invite the two young people to dinner, had my wife and me, cooks and maids in those days, all very elegant in a modest way (Donna with money in the background, I believe), the newlyweds arriving hand-in-hand at the doorstep and disappointed, politely, at being separated at table, he between Donna and my wife and she, Meg, between X and myself.

All four of us older, but not by much—as *we* understood much—ten or fifteen years, maybe twenty. Anyway, a good bit farther along the road than Tuckwell, farther up the tricky ladder. His stint in the Navy set him back but it certainly wasn't lost time for him because, on shore leave in some dim port he ran into an archeological troupe from some American university and fell in love with anthropology. Maybe a year or two somewhere else, I don't remember. All kinds of credentials, smart, presentable enough in every way, and yet somehow a whisper of small-town. You could hardly spot it, maybe nobody else did. No sign they did. Or cared. The ladies obviously found him charming ("Sweet smile," my wife said later—three times), Donna showing, it seemed to me, a glimmer of interest in how he viewed the twelve or so years between them—a much bigger span looking up from twenty-eight than down from forty.

And something of the same on our side of the table between young Mrs. Tuckwell—Meg, possibly twenty-three—and X and me, a much bigger span, maybe twenty-five or thirty years, enough to make us insist on "Tom" and "Norman" (no trouble about "Meg," a daughter's age if we had had one). X behaving like a boy walking on his hands before the new girl in town—talking about the *Oedipus* that the Thespians had staged the night before: "The good King just overreacted. He should have called in the Royal Shrink, who would have assured him every man wants to kill his father so he can marry his mother" (Meg smiling at her wedding ring as she tried to listen to our dated patter through wanting to hear what this Mrs. X was presuming to say to her husband). And tolerant of my own exhibitionism when I threw in my uncalled-for bit about "You seek and you find but what you find is not what you were seeking." — A smallish fair-haired girl with the sort of unconscious self-confidence you get from a mixture of approvals in your backgouund, social and personal. Friends, yes; lovers no; would-be lovers, *mille é tre*. Truthful eyes; something in them my wife's didn't have, and certainly Donna's didn't, maybe something you naturally outgrow.

I remember glancing at X for his impression if his manner showed it. He seemed attentive to what she was saying but his old eyes had wandered to her throat and a chain of some sort round her neck with a pendant falling between her breasts, and I thought he is only half hearing her and I couldn't blame him—breasts that might have been tailored to her measure and that she accepted and wore with the sort of unconscious satisfaction I used to feel in the days when I had my suits custom made not lifted from the rack and never quite right. I caught myself thinking they must have traveled with her Oscar boy-friend, nursed him on the high seas and brought him back to her safe and sound—and smiling.

As anybody knows, and certainly X and Donna had been out in the great world long enough to know, you are wasting your time to fall in love with someone, or even think you might, until the someone stops feeling deprived at being unable to hold the other-one's hand beneath the table. Which I thought that evening might not be for some time. They weren't exactly amateurs among the pros but the thought did occur to me the day my wife and I joined the gallery on donated tickets and followed a few holes of the U.S. Open not far away. I mean some amateurs are better than some pros, so there is no built-in disparagement in my thinking of Lieutenant and Mrs.

Tuckwell—Oscar and Meg—as amateurs.

They found a small garage-apartment not far from the Graduate School, Donna and Meg found it, Lieutenant Oscar diving into his curriculum like a swimmer at a tournament hitting the roped-off lanes of the pool. We had them over one evening out of politeness, just the two of them (still holding hands, nourishing each other like Siamese twins), and they had us back after a time, just my wife and me. They spoke of Donna and X, casually. He did: "The Doctor runs a tight ship," she quiet, smiling at her free hand.

And that was just about the end of it for us. A word about them now and then from X when our paths crossed and I asked. "Sharp. Top-quality work. You don't tell him twice."

"You think he'll swing his Doctor's," not so much a question, which seemed already answered by his tone, but to keep him talking because he seemed through with it.

"If he doesn't sprain something up here" (waving at his head). "I told him once to ease up, take his wife up to the Big City for a week. He said, 'Later.' I think Meg's not too happy about it all. His wife, Meg."

"Yes, I remember Meg. But he won't let up?"

"He's on to something he's trying to prove for his dissertation, something about frogs and salt water. First thing I told him, of course, was keep it quiet, don't tell *anybody*, not even your wife. I said, 'There're pirates on this ocean, Lieutenant,' and he said, Yes, he knew. I think I know where he's headed but I'm keeping out of it."—I told him he was quite right.

I saw Tuckwell in the cafeteria one lunchtime, across the room, he didn't see me. He was there with two young people. I suppose from the lab. Later when I looked again he was alone and I thought I would stop by and speak on my way out even though he was intent on jotting in a notebook—without glasses, prompting me to take mine off and wipe them on a paper napkin (very good for cleaning glasses). When I had them on and could see him again the situation at his table had changed considerably. He was talking across the notebook to Donna. Or listening, smiling a little, *the* smile. I had never seen her in the cafeteria before, though of course she had every right to be there if she wanted to, faculty wife, and probably there meeting X anyway; dressed very fittingly for a visit among us academic diners, ornaments ('accessories,' as they call them) held to a minimum, but still more decorative than the general run of our lady professors.

I thought he seemed rather impatient at being interrupted, tapping his pencil on the notebook page, one end then the other—but listening, attending, nodding, bringing up a smile, the smile. I left them; I had a graduate seminar coming up. The door was in another direction but I think I might have walked past their table without catching their eye, hers anyway. I thought X would be joining them any minute and I considered waiting outside to have a word with him, it had been weeks since I had seen him. Just as well I didn't wait; he was at a symposium on the Coast, Berkeley, had connections at Berkeley, did his training there.

Not long after that I had a phone call from an old student of mine in Washington who had gone up the ladder to a very good thing on the staff of a highly respected scientific magazine (some Government tie-in, I don't know what—neither here nor there). He said it looked as if they might be in the market one day soon for a young Ph.D. in Anthropology and if I knew of somebody there at the University to let him know. They had all kinds of applicants of course but a Doctor's from Princeton would carry weight. They were putting in for a foundation grant that would cover most of the salary; he mentioned a figure but I've forgotten—except that I said I'd like to apply for the job, which made us both laugh.

Of course I thought of Tuckwell, though he was hardly in line for it with almost another year to go before he would meet the requirements; the opening might well not exist by the time he got the doctorate. I hadn't seen him all winter, in fact not since the moment with Donna in the cafeteria. We had asked him and Meg over to dinner once but they were busy and we dropped it; too many years between us anyway.

But one morning in spring I happened to meet X coming out of the Chemistry Building and we talked for a few minutes on the steps.

He seemed in good shape but he surprised me by lighting a cigarette. He had given up smoking long ago; as I had too, shaking my head when he held out the pack. I asked about Tuckwell, mentioned the opening in Washington, or what had been an opening, possibly filled by then.

He knew about it. Tuckwell knew about it, had talked to him, wanted his advice on applying for it. "What was my frank opinion—as if I'd give any other kind—on his doctorate going through? Fair? Good? Excellent? It rather annoyed me, Norman; pushing me to some sort of commitment six months before he'd finished the disquisition. I told him it was the Board's decision, not mine. He pressed me, not one to underestimate himself, you know. Asked if I would feel like backing him. I said that depended on the paper, and he said with his little sideways laugh, 'It's a good paper.'"

I asked if he had seen any of it and he said, A few parts. "Essentially, trying to show that tadpoles will grow from eggs whose nucleus has been replaced by the nucleus of an adult frog's skin cell. Fair enough, if he can do it.

And somebody else doesn't do it first.—How's your wife?"

Of course I said, Fine, and asked after Donna. It surprised me a little that he just nodded (though that was really adequate as response), stepped on his cigarette, said we must have lunch one day soon, he would call me (the ready-to-wear dismissal) and hurried off—a little testy, I thought, a little up-tight? Maybe not.

The first I heard of Tuckwell's trip to the Washington people was in a note from my old student. They liked him; rather more than like him, were impressed. Tuckwell had mentioned me, and X of course, but said he had come down on his own; hadn't consulted anybody. Face-to-face was best, he said. They could see him, and also he could see them—good-natured about it, easy, but meaning it too. He wanted to know about housing and my friend drove him round in his neighborhood. Tuckwell said there would be three of them, one about two feet long if they hired him in the fall. Very pleasant guy; they liked him. The Foundation had come through very handsomely with a grant, as my friend put it, "to defray costs 1 Ph.D. in Anthropology''; they were meeting in a week or so to go through the applications and make a choice.

My friend thought it would be a good idea if Tuckwell met "the Chief" (and "the Chief" met Tuckwell) but he was out of town until the next day. So Tuckwell spent the night, my friend put him up, Tuckwell phoning home to Meg, then phoning the lab and leaving word with Paula to tell Dr. X he would be absent the next morning but would be on hand early in the afternoon—confident, but conscientious too (and insisting on paying for the calls, nothing much, a dollar to two).

Then X gets the message and calls Donna from the lab that he will be detained at the office and not to hold dinner for him, he will get a snack at the cafeteria. And don't wait up for him; he couldn't tell how long this might go on. Then he calls Meg, asks to speak to Oscar, is told Oscar is in Washington, and asks Meg if he may stop in for a minute on his way home to leave some notes for Oscar. "But certainly. How thoughtful of you!" says little wife to husband's boss.

And, "Certainly, oh what a nice idea!" when

he finishes his drink and proposes "driving out for a bite" at a new place one of his people has told him of.

Incidentally, he laid all this before me later on the plane to Georgia, really upset and finding me, I suppose, perhaps the only one knowing everybody concerned. I listened, all ears as many little details fell into the blank spaces in what I already knew, or guessed. He wanted to talk, needed to, might have gone to a shrink if as a scientist he hadn't been contemptuous. And he probably felt, too, that I would understand, sensing, I believe, my own down-the-years love—not quite love, of course, just a seedling—for the fresh, smooth-cheeked, quickly smiling Mrs. Tuckwell, Meg (a teetering smile, as if waiting).—But talking to me came later. Our paths didn't usually cross.

It doesn't take much imagination to see the attraction, Meg half his age (or less) wanting to please the boss to further husband's career, rather flattered too by the old man's attention to her as individual, possibly concerned in her own mind that her newly started pregnancy might spoil her appeal, not aware, I should say, that biology had more than taken care of that by toning her cheeks and hair and body the way a musician perfects the pitch of his violin before a recital. She could never have looked better.

For him there were other angles too, as he admitted later (hurrying over them). He had put this and that together and come out with Donna, turning forty, handsome as ever in his eyes, or more so, but wanting reassurance from someone besides him, wanting some fresher proof of her appeal than his fifteen-year-old attentions. Not the first time he had ticked off such guesses, her forays usually leading to jealousy on his part and after a while ending in renewed devotion (possibly supplemented by inherent surprises in the forays themselves), and back to forbearance and a not-intolerable makeshift ecstasy. He had even been half prepared to find she wasn't home when he phoned from the lab, had gone to Washington with Tuckwell; ridiculous of course but jealousy paints with a nonobjective brush. He was not at all prepared, the next time Tuckwell's name came up between them, to find she was indignant: "He is annoying me, this young man. Can you imagine!"

X making light of it with, "Well, after all, baby, you're quite a temptation, you know."

She said, Thank you, but she hadn't descended to high-school dropouts yet, and he shouted, "Dropout!" and they both laughed—the clouds circling round and away.

He didn't quite believe her; she was blowing up something insignificant, misinterpreting something. But he did believe there might have been something to blow up, to misinterpret, and it changed the way he felt about Meg, or not the way he felt but the way he might express it. If the boy had the nerve, the self-confidence, to "annoy" X's wife then X would have the nerve to do the same to the boy's (not that he hadn't thought of it before—dreamed of it).

But of course it came to nothing, except that it created a sort of frosty coating over the mentor-student relationship with Tuckwell—husband and obstacle to X's interest in Meg (which grew stronger against the impediment), and also an object of jealousy because of what X believed was Donna's unconscious (or not unconscious?) attraction to the "dropout."

Anyway, off again to the West Coast, taking Donna with him this time, and during the week he was away Tuckwell got the job, phoning me in his exuberance. They had just called him with the news: formal papers in the mail, sign, two witnesses, notary, return one copy, send photocopy of the dissertation registered mail as soon as confirmed.

Then he and Meg to Washington to find accomodations, finding something—McLean, I believe—taking it on a three-year lease for occupancy immediately after his appearance before the Board; back to the University and coming to my office, both of them, to thank me for my help, I trying to explain I had done nothing, but getting a bottle out of a bottom drawer and pouring us all a congratulatory glass. In another week he had turned in his dissertation, packed up and left; I stopped by their apartment as they were phoning for a taxi. When I offered to shake hands with Meg she flung her arms round my neck and kissed me on the mouth. I remember the feel of her lips.

Sarah-Wesley said, "You loved the woman yourself, you rascal," the Doctor lifting his hand in a gesture that might have been a mild denial or just a signal he hadn't finished yet, Ray mumbling something trivial while his thoughts adjusted not so much to the doctor's being in love with Meg, obvious enough, but to the possibility the doctor and "colleague" were one and the same—the mate with elastic strides tailored to fit the movement of the deck like a circus performer on his bouncing wire, ignoring the passengers as usual (as if it were Rule One in his Service Manual), taking the companionway up to the bridge two steps at a time, the cat trailing like a dinghy. In love with Meg at the time and thought he still was, the idea giving Ray a shock of recognition like passing someone on the street who reminds you of someone else, of yourself indeed, yourself distorted in the Fun-House mirror; of himself being in love with Claudia once and thinking he still was, her voice coming through her letters, "They mowed the wheat below us yesterday, what a glorious smell!"—The Doctor clarifying his lifted hand with, "That's not quite all of it."

(THE DOCTOR'S COLLEAGUE'S TALE—CONCL.)

The baby was born, a boy, in McLean a week after they settled in, the move itself, new friends, new surroundings and all that helping to bring it on I'd say, let the gynecologists smile. Everything fine, except certification hadn't come through; he had taken the two five-hour finals and the two-hour oral, handed in his dissertation and was ready to come up any day at X's notification for the final public oral. After another week he wrote X a polite note: he didn't want to seem impatient, he knew such things took time, but the people down there had asked him again and it was a little embarrassing. They had taken him on the strength of it and were getting a little uneasy.

When he got no answer in ten days he told Meg he was going up there and try to hurry it up. She suggested phoning Dr. X; "So much easier, honey. And cheaper!" He said, Seeing his face was as important as hearing his voice; nevertheless he phoned.

But Dr. X was "not in the office this morning." "Is this Paula?"

"Yes it is, Dr. Tuckwell."

"Paula, please ask him to call me tonight after six," looking down at their new number and giving it to her. She said she was sorry but they didn't expect him back until Monday, he was on the West Coast. "Well, ask him to call me as soon as he gets back. Important, Paula."

But he didn't call, and when Tuckwell reached him on the phone Monday afternoon he said only, Such things took time you know, tell those people down there to keep their pants on. "There's possibly one little snag, Lieutenant."

"Snag!"

"I can't tell you any more right now—"

"What do you mean, snag?"

"I'll call you in a day or two when I know something. Do I have your number? Yes, Paula says we have."

But the "people down there" had got the grant on the basis of the Ph.D. and they phoned him—the Chief's assistant did—and most courteously asked about it. They needed some credentials to show the Foundation office; would really like to provide them with a copy of the certificate, "just as a matter of form. Let us have it as soon as you can, Doctor, it's getting a little awkward for us."

The rest of it seemed to happen all at once, though of course it took hours, took all of a beautiful October Thursday—the early call from X, "Some not-good news, old fellow. Looks like a guy at Berkeley beat you to it," waiting a minute, getting only a dead silence and going on, "same problem, same theory, practically the same demonstration. Happens all the time, of course. Two people, miles apart, never heard of each other, pop up one day with the same idea. Happens all the time. Darwin and What's-his-name, you remember—"

"You mean—"

"Trouble is the *Journal's* publishing this guy's paper in the next—"

"You mean I don't get my Doctor's?"

"Not at all, Oscar. You just don't' get it on the basis of this dissertation—"

"I just start all over again!"

"It's a lot simpler the second go-round, Oscar—"

"Wait a minute! Who is this guy? You know this guy?"

"Not really. No."

"Isn't Berkeley your school?"

"Now wait a minute yourself, Oscar—"

"You didn't steer him on to my idea?"

"Now hold on, Lieutenant!"

"Nobody else knew, I haven't told a living soul—"

"These things happen, I tell you. Happen all the time—"

"You gave him my idea—"

"You're insane!" And the line went dead.

X was crossing the yard to his car when Tuckwell tramped through a bed of late flowers at a corner of the house, bareheaded, unshaved, rumpled collar, service pistol heavy in his hand. X drew back rigid against the side of the car, so surprised he couldn't find a directive of any sort, his mind like a jostled tray of tools; should he speak, say something, just to break the silence? caution the boy, warn him? Beg him? No words ready that seemed to fit, and no physical movement, no way open to escape with the car door against his back, a thought taking shape in his head that any move to duck and run, or even any spoken words would be enough to break some delicate balance in the air between them, trip some spring, all the choices seeming to cancel one another and leave him standing there, chest square to the front, staring at the pale young man ten feet away, and continuing to stare without moving, unable to move, as the young man put the pistol muzzle in his mouth like a fat cigar and pushed the trigger with his thumb.

"You mean this Professor X got jealous and—"

I told him there was no reason he should go to Georgia for the funeral—he was badly shaken—but he wouldn't listen, and I went with him, just the two of us. We kept out of the way, stood off among the trees, the oleanders, some white camellias, didn't speak to anybody, sign any book. Saw Meg from a distance, blank, dazed as if a bright light had flashed into her eyes; didn't speak to her (she wouldn't have known it if we had), flew back that afternoon.

"You mean this Professor—"

"I've told you all I know—except she married again, an Englishman trading in sugar with a plantation in Barbados. One reason I agreed to make the talks at the College. She'll be surprised. She doesn't know I'm coming.''

Ray heard himself exclaim in not much more than a whisper to himself, ''Doesn't know you're coming? She'll hear about it through the College.''

''Not likely. But even if she does?—Oh, I won't just walk in the door. I'll ask here and there, size up the situation. If I decide I'm not intruding, I'd like to see her. It's been twenty years, more than twenty. I don't like to add it up.''

Ray said, ''She won't be the woman you remember,'' as if speaking into a mirror, giving Geltstein (and himself) an excuse for changing his mind, but the Doctor only said, ''Even so?'' and after a pause, ''A later bud on the same stem?'' smiling a little to dilute the sentimentality then going on that he once knew a man who said he told a woman he loved her more than when she was beautiful. ''She was indignant. He said if she had had a frying pan he would have been a dead duck. Beauty matters more than love—to some of them . . . .''

Voice fading out for Ray under the temptation of recalling to the Doctor his cautionary "what you find is not what you were searching for," but changing his mind at realizing it might apply to himself as well: two men each looking for a woman he had loved.—Or was he looking for the man who had loved her?

In any case, the Doctor's planning to see Meg seemed to strengthen Ray's weakening resolve to seek out Claudia. If the Doctor was willing to chance it, determined to, why not Ray? Twenty years, for the Doctor? Closer to thirty for himself—since the train and the pulsing brakes and the door shutting, the snap of the latch saying, "End," like a voice. And close to two since *"Walter Motlow, in Afghanistan"* and wondering through a restless night's half-sleep after seeing it if the news might be excuse enough for writing her, breaking the long silence. And waking to realize he couldn't write her: *"Claudia Baird of Austin, Texas"* didn't mean she was living there now; and even if she were he had no mailing address.

And without deciding anything, whether he would write her even if he could—only remembering the petty swindle Emily said she sometimes resorted to if she needed a far-away address quickly—he dialed "Directory

Assistance'' in Austin and asked for the phone number of ''a Mrs. Walter Motlow.''

A pleasant un-Southern voice said after a pause as if for thinking (or for touching the keys of a computer), ''Five-one-two, four-five-nine, four-zero-one-five.''

He said, ''Is that the Mrs. Motlow at two-three-one University Place?''

''No sir, the only Mrs. Walter Motlow we have is at seven-four-three Pedernales Drive.''

''Thank you, Directory Assistance.''

''Our pleasure, sir, have a nice evening.''

''The same to all of you, miss.''

And he wrote her. Six lines of insipid condolence that he rewrote as many times, not reminiscent, not asking her to remember—except in the full-of-time ''Always'' that he ended with—mailed it with no return address on the envelope for fear it would come back unopened. Week after week until nearly two months had passed, then eight lines: she was busy with selling her house, planning to move into a retirement community, ''meaning a place for old folks'' (Isabel's plan, Isabel's words—and maybe his own plan too, maturing in the dark); ''costly but very nice.'' Cool, occupied, looking-another-way; except, possibly, the glancing-back "Always, C"?

Drop it? Did he really want her to meet young-Edward-("Eddie")-plus-thirty-years? Plus present-day infirmities (physical and possibly mental)? And yet with Isabel the old years had glowed with a quiet richness over his seeing her again; old years without the intensity of the Claudia years, but reassuring in the values that remained, the risen-to-the-surface creamy values—at the airport watching her mount the landing stairs to her plane with more alacrity than his game leg would have allowed him, in his mind Ora Mae's staggering "Why don't you marry Mr. Edward, Miss Isabel?" turning into "Why don't you marry Miss Claudia, Mr. Edward?" and bringing back to him the web of imagined affinities, some of which might have weathered the years. And he wrote her again, after waiting ten days for pride's sake, a factual noncommittal note, longer than the first but not saying much, a tentative holding out his hand in the way he had seen his neighbor's children tempting their rabbit ("Rabbit E. Lee" by name).

No answer. Weeks growing into months—

months filled with the night-and-day nursing of their Fall List (three titles); flyers to compose and fling out into the void, review copies to the mighty (who would ignore them—no fear of publisher pausing at luncheon table with, "What's the matter with you people over there, can't you read?"); authors unhappy at dustjackets, at advertising, at the inevitable typo, at the Conspiracy of Indifference (one of them grumbling, "Samizdat!" for the way the Press was "concealing" his work); publisher-editor-stenographer-shipping-clerk filling a dribble of orders in the mail—not even an order from Texas.

Then one morning a thin envelope with a British-looking stamp canceled in San Juan de Pinos: Four lines on stationery of *Mrs. Martha Freeland* (crossed out but with a phone number showing); she was spending a few weeks with a daughter who had taken a sublet in the hills outside of San Juan. "Grandchildren under foot! Can you imagine? If you can, please don't.—Toujours, C."

And he had told the other half of the Press to expect him in two weeks (catching himself on the brink of "with a new wife"), gone to a travel agency and asked if there were boats to San Juan de Pinos.

"Boats!"

"Yes, I don't fly well." (And want some time to think, to consider,—to maybe re-consider.)

And the ship still with him on the hotel porch as the muscles in his shoulders seemed to rock against the moving chair-back, his mind to rock between the black taxi driver talking to someone at the foot of the steps and the blistered castaways jabbering in the rowboat—and on to the jabbering hour on shore in Bridgetown with Pyt the diver and the pickle-man from Colorado who said, "Book-writing is an all-right business if it pays off," the three of them wandering about the docks, the vast contemptuous heat like a motionless storm (Geltstein off with a wave in a taxi), the ladies doing the shops along Victoria Street—

"Pardon, sir," from "Thomas" with a tray of ice and scotch whisky; "the lady phoned to tell the gentleman not much longer. To bring him 'something else to wait with,'" setting the tall glass on the arm of the chair and removing the empty one.

"Thank you, Thomas,"—none of it seeming

to break into the streets of Bridgetown and Pyt shouting, "Come along, Captain!" waving an invitation to join them at the Captain on the steps of the Harbor Master's office, cap on the back of his head, pipe in his teeth, looking as uncomfortable ashore as the boats in the bay aground at low tide.

No answer, and they took a table at the nearest cafe—the *Café Divine*—to get out of the sun, a table by an open window for the air moving in from the water, Pyt looking out at the flock of off-the-vertical masts and, when his drink had come, swallowing an inch or two.

THE DIVER'S TALE

Low tide once in Marriaqua Town, in the bay and in myself. Would have jumped off the dock if there had been more water. A man came up behind me, said somebody told him I was a diver. I said I might be. I had been working on a job out of Key West. The boss thought he had found the *Señora d'Atocha*. I went down three times, had a good look. Picked up a bagful of coins. Found four solid silver bars, managed to bring one up. Weighed eighty pounds. ''It's the *Atocha*!'' says he. ''No sir, she's too small.'' He kicked me out. Wanted her to be the *Atocha*. I hooked a ride to Marriaqua where I knew a shady lawyer from back home in Louisiana—-not Louise-iana, named for Louis.

This man, smelling like a shrimp boat, asked me if I was looking for a job, ''something special?'' I said I might be. ''Depends.''

''You ever see anything like this?'' says he, digging into his pants pocket and bringing up a coin worn almost smooth. He wouldn't give it to me to hold but he let me look at it in his hand. A gold doubloon with a profile that might have been the King of Spain on one side and on the other a pressing of the True Cross and under it, very small, you could hardly make it out, ''Colon, 1621.''

I said, ''Where'd you steal this?''

He said he had a ''pile of 'em.'' Said he and his partner found them while fishing for turtles on a reef south of Cuba, ''never mind which reef.'' Said the wreck lay on her side in four fathoms with a heavy current, most of it half buried in silt. They figured she must be the *Margarita* that people talked about; what looked like an anchor sticking up not far off. "Had six prongs."

I said, "Ain't no such anchor," to him, but to myself I said this guy's on to something; I'd been down enough to see those six-pronged anchors, three flukes each side of the shank. I said I had other pots on the fire but what was his proposition.

He said shares, everybody got an equal share, and I said, "Who's 'everybody'?" He said there'd be him and his partner and two others to help. I said, "A five-way split, me doing all the work, breaking all the bones!" He said it was his boat, and I said it was my neck, "$500 and half of what I find. If I don't find nothing, just $500." He spit three inches short of my shoes and walked off, jingled his ducats or whatever they were and walked off.

And I walked off too. But that "Colon, 1621" followed me like a stray dog. Hurricanes are down my alley: "July, stand by; August, come it must; September, remember." 1621 was the year of the big blow. Or it might have been 1622, I wasn't sure. The ships came in from Spain, you know, maybe picked up a few pearls at Cartagena, sailed on to Porto Bello and Colon and loaded up with silver from Peru, gold from Chile, minted at Colon or Lima. Then northeast on the Trades and into the Gulf until they hit the Stream, north on the current round the end of Cuba and up the Florida coast, then east for home. If the Saints held back the hurricanes. And held off the robbers, Trent, Black Beard, Lafitte and the rest. They gathered at Havana, the merchant ships; waited to make up a convoy, maybe waited for a galleon like the *Margarita* or the *Madre de Dios*—a police escort.

But I'm getting off the track.

I went to see my lawyer friend, needed to talk to somebody it didn't much matter who. He had run into a little trouble back home in Pineville, nothing much. DUIs used to come to him, not everyday drunks, big-time drunks, Country-Club drunks, sheriff in the parking lot Saturday night waiting for them. His fee was a couple of hundred to get the hook out of their mouth that he split 50-50 with the sheriff; one thing and another. Managed to get himself disbarred and skipped out for foreign parts, for Marriaqua eventually.

And landed on both feet. He had a boat. "Cup defender," he said, whatever that means. Bought it cheap. The bank had it up for sale to settle an estate. Schooner-rigged, with a back-up diesel. Didn't look like a boat that would be running cocaine, heroin and all that.

He said he was busy; said there were a thousand reefs "south of Cuba." "Needle in a haystack." Said to feel around, see if I could run into something with a little meat on it, said to try the Library, he had heard they had a file of old newspapers that went "way back."

I remember watching a redhead buzzard through a Library window, slipping and sliding on a tin rooftree trying to get a grip with his claws, and me there inside clawing into journals, histories, diaries, microfilms of letters, finding nothing—nothing with a scrap of meat on it. Then one day hitting on a quote from the *Marriaqua Gazette* of August 1622 that mentioned a "reception by the Governor for the Captain and officers of the *Madre de Dios*," banquet, ball, cockfights, the works (I could feel the hair on my head lifting up). She was sailing on the morning tide, headed home for Cadiz.

Cadiz? Why not Havana to join the convoy? And yet she might have sailed "for Cadiz" by way of Havana. The quote ended with, "She is believed to have aboard 47 tons of gold and silver in ingots and coin minted at Colon."

I followed such a hint on to the next issue of the *Gazette.* A three-inch paragraph said, "In this town, the fairest of all the English plantations, every house within view is leveled." (It hit me like a crack of lightning.) "All the vessels in the harbor are drove ashore and one Bristol ship overset and lost. At St. Iago de la Vega the rector reads prayers to keep up some show of religion among a most ungodly and debauched people . . . ." No mention of the *Madre* except indirectly in the last line: "Many ships are feared lost along the coast of Cuba or in the Windward Passage to the east, only 40 miles wide and directly in the course of the storm, the most violent in recollection."

Which way did she sail? West on the Trades, bound for Havana and the convoy? Or did she say to hell with a convoy and take the short cut due north through the Windward Passage? She was a battleship, didn't need a convoy, could take care of herself—

Frank Hardly breaking in with, "All right, all right! Did you get the loot, the moola?"

We headed northeast for the Windward Passage, all sails set, the lee-rail almost level with the foam. Five of us aboard not counting the Portuguese steward in a flower-pot hat and his black wife the cook. We were drinking champagne about twelve o'clock on the second day, arguing about how far into the Passage she might have got before the hurricane struck her; you couldn't say for sure because we didn't know what time she had sailed. "Morning tide" didn't help much. But we did agree the storm would have driven her west, on to the Cuba reefs (which fitted in pretty well with what the fisherman told me), and that was where we were headed.

I was checking out my gear when I noticed the sky was fading out under a misty scud. To windward the squall had already whitened the near sea and was coming on with a strange and dismal sound. "Down mainsail! Down staysail!" And the great sail came down with a run and fell half overboard. I could see the steersman clinging to the spokes, face as gray as the wet sail. The squall fell in a solid mass of wind and rain and we stooped under the blow and wild noise. The foresail boom tore apart the last strands of the sheet and crashed to leeward. The ship leaped up into the wind and righted and the peak and throat halyards began to run—

"All right, all right! But did you—"

—for some ten minutes more she careened under the squall and then, like a freight train slamming past you and gone, the squall blew by, the wind dropped into light airs and the sun came out. We secured the foresail boom, set hands at the pumps. Somebody said, "What's that over there!" It was the black tower of a submarine, Akula Class, dripping white sea-water down the sides. "Hooray! Glory be! Give us a hand. We're in trouble!" everybody waving, dancing around.

We must have scared her. She submerged while we were yelling. Headed west—

All of them turning as the bartender cried, "Ah, the Captain!" raising one hand in a high salute and reaching with the other into his basket of limes; going on to squeeze out a tall lime drink, mumbling, "Never touch a drop," to the three or four on the bar stools who obviously did, the Captain crossing the room, sitting down with his back to the door and tapping up the visor of his cap in a gesture of dropping anchor. When the bartender brought his lime drink he acknowledged it with a nod, adding other nods in silent answer to "How've you been, Captain?" and such greetings, waved at the table with, "Shipmates of mine," and seemed to feel that took care of everything, hoped it did, obviously thinking of something else.

Which came out clear enough when after a minute he said, "That no-good out there," stirring the lime drink with a disdainful first finger, "you saw him. Takes me back to Oslo. Father's Oslo."

Ray had hardly noticed him, beyond thinking, "Another one." Plenty of "no-goods" in harbor towns—a man close to forty, shirt and pants and broken shoes as run-down as paint on a tramp steamer. But he wondered if the man wasn't more than just "another one'' to the Captain to make him think of Oslo, Father's Oslo. ''Brought us all to the USA, the Promised Land, but couldn't get Oslo out of his mind. Talk for hours about the Navigation School in his day. Four years as seaman to be eligible. Then ten months at school and you can take the Mate's Examination,'' stopping to hold out a crooked wet finger to the small gray bird that had landed on the table for cracker crumbs, offering the finger, not insisting, the bird ignoring him, busy with the crumbs.

''If you pass you're eligible for a third-mate's berth. If you can find one. Two years as third mate and you go back and work a year to take the Master's Examination. Pass it and you get your Master's License, good as long as you stay out of trouble. Eight years from able seaman to Master. And more likely ten to twelve the way things work out, ships not just moored there waiting for you to come aboard. You can have a Master's License and can't find a ship to master. In that case if you're smart you take what you can find and sail as mate,'' ignoring the bird which, as if interested, had hopped up on the knuckle of his thumb. ''Like Wagman, Master's License and no ship, waiting for a break, a shift in the wind. You go with a big company if you can. In bad times they can find a place for a good man on another ship. Small company folds, sells out and you start over again. That man out there had a Master's License'' (moving his thumb and the bird hopping to the window-sill and flying away). ''Shipped as third mate on the *Marta S. deWaal,* 5,000 tons, bound for Hamburg with iron ore from Cyprus. Gale in the North Sea. Engines old and weak, speed checked, lost steerageway, she wouldn't answer. Breakers up ahead, first time I'd seen them from the deep-water side, jumping like white horses. Seven men lost with the ship, thought one was the mate until five minutes ago. . . .''

The man walking in the door, standing a minute to look about, then coming over to the table and leaning on the back of a vacant chair as if he were tired and saying, ''Captain, have you got a berth on the *Lindvagen* for an able seaman?'' as though knowing the answer. Or the sort of answer it would be, because he didn't seem surprised when the Captain pushed aside his lime drink, got up, walked over to the cashier, paid out some money and left the room.

They found him at a corner of the Park talking through the din of motor horns with Mrs. Hardly (LaVerne) and the young women from Mobile, each with parcels of little favors and decorations for the Christmas party, Preacher Bickle snapping pictures of them from a bench in the shade—until the camera was snatched from his neck by three men in khaki jackets with badges inside the lapels and he was marched away between them toward the Harbor Master's office, the Captain mumbling, "Soviet agent." "Captain! It couldn't be!" "They're everywhere—"

"Excuse me, sir," from a short black man at the top of the porch steps, a taxi-driver's cap on the back of his head with an oval "No. 17" pinned to the band. "The lady? Mr. Hugh Jim say take the lady where she want to go." "And you can do that?" "Oh yes. Mr. Hugh Jim speak, we jump."

Ray told him the lady would be back shortly, "Any minute now," beginning to wonder if she would be—appearing out of nowhere two hours ago disappearing into another nowhere now—the driver sitting down on a top step with his cap on a knee as if used to waiting.

And Ray returning through the silence, the hot silence laced with city sounds like bright threads, to the girls from Mobile under the Christmas lanterns and one of them (Becky, he thought, prompted by the other) saying, "Yes, well," and after a glance at her fingernails as if checking her notes, "This friend of mine married an advertising man in New York . . . ."

THE YOUNG WIFE'S TALE

She met him at an office party. He wasn't with her magazine but he sold ads for a record company the magazine did business with and somebody brought him. A black-haired man about thirty-five, not very tall, as I remember. Wore glasses—thin glass that needed a polishing—wore them in a friendly way as if he had worn them all his life. They gave him a serious look but he was really quite amusing. Stories about the advertising business. Said you could sell people anything if you wanted to spend the money, said he'd really like to live in Utah and raise honeybees.

I stayed with them once for two or three days. In New York to buy some new clothes, expensive ones, forget my new divorce and the handsome wretch who asked me for it. Slept on their sofa. A small third-floor walkup on 11th Street. I don't think I was much trouble and, for me, it was a joy to be with them, to be in the midst of a marriage that worked. Not demonstrative about it—oh, holding hands, yes, and really meaning the kisses when they met or separated, but comfortable with each other, considerate, watching for little ways to please. A smooth marriage. I saw her take off his glasses once, polish them and hook them back over his ears.

No children though they had been married three or four years when I was there. Didn't want children. She had a good job, liked the people, good pay, and he made as much or more. They talked about moving uptown. I went with her one lunch time to see a place on East 74th Street, larger, much more expensive but that didn't bother her. "We can handle it," she said. "We have a plan." She knew a married woman in her office who said she and her husband had saved a great chunk of taxes by getting a divorce in December and getting married again in January. The taxes they paid as singles, with single deductions and all, came out to much less than being married and using a joint return.

She said they had talked it over, my friend and her husband, figured it up and down, right and left, and decided they would do that too. With what they saved they could easily manage the uptown apartment, more convenient for both, closer to their offices, no subway, an easy walk.

They had got a young lawyer whose firm did some work for the magazine to draw up the divorce papers, simple enough, uncontested, she and her husband signing in the lawyer's office and going out hand-in-hand. A few days later she took a couple of hours off and met him and the lawyer at the courthouse, and by twelve o'clock everything was done and she and her ex-husband threw their arms about each other and kissed for so long the judge whacked his gavel and said, "Next case!" but smiled a little.

They separated on the courthouse steps; he had an appointment on Vesey Street and she had already been away from her desk nearly half the morning. "Good-by, honey," she said, "I'll pick up something special on the way home we can have for supper." He said, "Fine, baby, I'll get a bottle of champagne.'' And they kissed again, a long kiss, she said, like the one five years before when they left the magistrate's office as man-and-wife.

She was a little late after the supermarket and wasn't surprised the apartment was lighted up when she opened the door. Or surprised he didn't answer her, ''I'm home, honey-bun!''; probably in the bathroom—maybe polishing his glasses to celebrate. But when she went to the bedroom closet to hang up her coat his suits were gone, his country jacket, his extra shoes. His pair of hairbrushes were gone off the bureau, not a shirt in the drawers, not a handkerchief, not a pair of socks.

She never saw or heard from him again.

Pyt said, ''Didn't the bastard even leave a note?'' and Becky said, ''No, but he did leave the bottle of wine, and she drank the whole thing, took it out of the fridge, popped the cork and drank the whole thing.—Where's Sarah-Wesley? Oh, there she is with Mr. Wagman.''

Frank Hardly said, ''Reminds me of the time I lost my wife. Remember, LaVerne?''

''Do I!''

THE PICKLE-MERCHANT'S TALE

Married five or six years, left the kids with her mother, drove in to Denver from Greeley—sixty miles—to take her to an eye man, do some errands, one thing and another.

We were already a little late for the eleven-o'clock appointment so I drove straight on into the middle of town and stopped in front of the doctor's office in one of the tall buildings, horns behind me like a flock of crows, a cop's whistle from somewhere. "Hotel! One o'clock!"—could hardly make her hear me for the racket (don't get to the city once a year, not then if I can help it).

First thing to do was park the car and I turned off the main street to find a garage, find one that wasn't full. Plenty of garages but all of them bursting. One guy was decent enough to lean out of his office window and say try two blocks down, turn left, just opened up, maybe got a space. It worked. They took the car, gave me a ticket, *Denver Auto Park, 80 Valmont St.* I said I'd want the car about four o'clock. "No problem!" Nice fellow. Mike. Looked like a stable-hand.

And a nice cool October day, sunny. I had some city errands to tend to, odds and ends, I don't remember. Walked up to the center of town, saw a winter jacket in a window, plaid, went in and bought it, I'm a fool for plaid, feeling good and all that, didn't need it. Wife waiting in the lobby, nice lunch. "What's that you've got?" Showed her the jacket. She shook her head. "All right, I'll return it." I didn't like it much myself on second look. She had to go back to the eye man and wind it up. "All right, meet me at the garage at 4:30 sharp. That'll get us home by dark." I showed her the ticket and she wrote down "Denver Auto Park, 80 Valmont St., 4:30."

We separated and I wandered about, drank a beer—maybe two—took the jacket to the store, *Homestake Clothiers.* They wanted to credit me and I wanted the cash. No smiles this afternoon, money headed the other way. They called the manager. He ended our back-and-forth talk by giving me the cash but it seemed to me later that this was where the fine fall day began to go wrong.

I walked on along the main street until I recognized the cross street where the garage was, but the street sign didn't say Valmont. It said Loretto Street. It made me a little dizzy; I said, "Hold everything now, Frank. Take a deep breath." I stopped a man, asked him where Valmont Street was.

"Valmont? Keep going, doc. It's a good ten blocks farther on, straight on."

But this was the street I had walked out of three hours before. Was I ready for the bin! I wasn't, though, because I couldn't help walking a few steps down this "Loretto Street" and in a minute there was the *Denver Auto Park*. "Sorry," the man said, Mike. "Planned to open up on Valmont, had my tickets all printed, couldn't throw'm away. Marked out 'Valmont' on a pile of tickets last night, so many cars this morning used them all up. Forgot to mark the one you got. Sorry." Young, nice guy, needed a haircut.

"Okay, but I told my wife to meet me at 80 Valmont."

"No problem. Take the car, drive over there, pick her up."

"Maybe I can catch her at the doctor's. Can I borrow your phone?"

"Help yourself."

Then it was, No sir, Mrs. Hardly has just left.—Did she say where she was going?—No sir. Some shopping I believe.—I see. Well, if she comes back or calls in please tell her it's Loretto Street where the car is, not Valmont.—Loretto Street, not Valmont. Yes sir, but we don't expect her back.—All right, but for crying out loud tell her if you get a chance.—Yes sir. Have a nice day.—Thank you.

And, "Thanks for the phone," to Mike the garage man. "How do I get to Valmont Street? My wife's going to Valmont, been there since 4:30." My watch said five after five.

"No problem. Drive up to the corner, take a left—if the cop ain't looking—go on about ten blocks and you come to Valmont. Eighty's to the left but you can't left so go on another block and do a right and a right and a—"

"Thanks. I'll find it. What do I owe you?"

"No charge. Sorry about the ticket, scratched out a lot of them, all printed up and everything, couldn't—"

"Okay. Thanks. Thanks, Mike." Nice guy.

Drove up to the main street, tried a left, cop whistled like a busted tire, "What's a matter with you, cowhand! Can't you read!'' straight on, then left, left, right, eight blocks, nine blocks, *Valmont*! like a gold nugget. ''NO TURN.'' Okay, ten blocks, right, right, right on Valmont. Nobody walking on Valmont, a dingy street, nobody waiting.

And no 80. The Rocky Mountain Pawn Shop at 76, then a brick wall, then a closed-up warehouse that might have been Mike's abandoned Auto Park, and 88. I tried to figure what she would do, walking ten blocks (or taking a taxi) and finding the address didn't exist. Alone in the city, knowing nobody. The sky clouding up over the mountains like rain. Or early snow. Home sixty miles away. I would have sat down on the curb and bawled.

But not, I figured, LaVerne. A strong woman. She would have gone in the pawn shop, looked in their telephone book, got the real address of the *Denver Auto Park* on Loretto and called a taxi. She was probably there already.

But when I went in the pawn shop and looked in the telephone book there was no ''Denver Auto Park.'' All right, just moved, new phone. She would call Information and get the new address. I asked the pawn-shop man if I could use his phone. "Local call?" says he. "I want to call Information." "Make it fast."

I told Information I wanted the phone number of the *Denver Auto Park* on Loretto Street, thinking then I would also call Mike to watch out for her and tell her I would be there in five minutes. "We have no phone listed under that name, sir," says Information.

Now look here! (to myself). How do we do this? If your shoelaces get crossed up you don't pull the strings into a hard knot. You slack off a little bit, you keep them loose. Okay, but they were already in a hard knot. And a cop outside the door was getting off his motorcycle. "Don't you see that yellow line!" "I've lost my wife, officer, and it's time we started home, past time, I was just borrowing a phone." "Get this car out of here!"

I drove up to the main street, did a right, drove past the doctor's building, thought she might be standing on the sidewalk. Drove on past the hotel. Saw a clock on a church, nearly six o'clock. Heavy traffic now. Lights green, lights red, wiped the sweat off my face at a red light. No left, did a right. Saw a sign, "Loretto Street," pulled up at the *Denver Auto Park,* Mike making change for somebody.

"Didn't find her?"

"Can I use your phone?"

"Help yourself."

I phoned the doctor's office, got a recording. Phoned the hotel. "Is my wife waiting there in the lobby?" "What's she look like?" I hung up. Who can say what his wife looks like? I walked up to the corner, no idea why, just to keep moving. Cop by a lamp post watching the traffic like it was a TV movie. I said, "Excuse me, officer, but I can't find my wife" (nutty thing to say but I was going nutty). Before he could say anything something caught his eye and he walked off, and I leaned against the lamp post and said aloud but just for myself, Now look here! slack off a little bit. Don't press the emergency button. She may be standing there by the pawn shop now, or sitting in a taxi (a long walk from the doctor's office).

I got the car from Mike and halfway to Valmont Street, on a main street in the midst of home-going traffic I thought I had better phone the pawn-shop man to watch out for her on the sidewalk and tell her to wait there, I was on the way. Plenty of space in front of a corner drug store and a phone booth and I pulled over and stopped. Before I could open the car door a motorcycle cop zipped up beside me, boiling. "Get this car out of here!" "My wife—" "Can't you read. NO PARKING ANY TIME." "I've lost my wife—" "Get it out!"

Pyt said, "Quite a pickle, Mr. Pickle!" and Ray said, "Let him finish," (seeking his wife, as the Doctor was seeking Meg, Ray seeking Claudia, Pyt himself seeking the rest of his sunken doubloons—and nobody, according to the Doctor, going to find just what he sought?).

I drove on. NO LEFT. NO TURN. busses, crowds waiting. Red light. Green light. Where was I going? Valmont? Loretto? Couldn't say. Car ahead made a right, I made a right. Green light, squawking horns behind me. And there she was! On a corner. She hadn't seen me. I slammed the horn, slammed it again. "Hey! Hey! You!*You*!"—I couldn't remember her name—

"But Edward, even if your company doesn't publish fiction you know people that do," the taxi slowing at a road fork, turning off into a dirt road slanted up the mountainside, hardly more than a trail. He said, Oh there were plenty of people who published fiction—sensing the old familiar situation taking shape again: eager writer, wary publisher, out-of-breath swimmer and just-in-time lifeguard (or seeming so to her, Janet Somebody, accounting for her troubling herself with someone her father's age), he lifting a hand at a far-off sound like faint thunder out of cotton-boll clouds that flashed him an uneasy picture of a road like this in a tropical cloudburst.

She said, "Drums," adding, "Tumbas. Pans," as if annoyed at his bringing up such irrelevances, then went on with what she was saying in a way that made him see Mary intent on finishing a seam in her sewing machine, "And besides, this isn't exactly fiction, not exactly."

He said, Most fiction wasn't "exactly fiction," his words bringing back to him his earlier thought that her book derived somehow from the "back country"—and might after all be of some interest to the Press? (the taxi striking a pothole as if to signal him a

No, the jolt throwing the side of her arm against him, flooding his mind with other arms, other responses, like far-away voices on turn-of-the-century phones, hardly recognizable).

"If you think it's any good you could send me to somebody. If it's no good you wouldn't have to. No obligation," touching the side of his hand as if to reassure him. He said he wouldn't have a chance to read it here, would only be on the Island a day or two, the words carrying a sort of negative that was like his crippled response to her touch. Leading him on to soften it a little with, "Tell me about your book," an invitation that was like offering a writer a chair whether you wanted him to sit down or not—and they always "sat down". Or like asking "What's his name?" of the fond mother, or "How old is he?" He knew from experience you needed to be prepared for a full answer.

But he wasn't ready for, "It's about what you will feel when you read it," laughing a little as if she had overdressed it and adding, "I'd have to recite the whole book to show you what I mean—not that I couldn't do that."

He said he would leave her his address, she could send it to him; doubting that she ever would and in any case postponing the need to sample it, dip into it, search about for a gentle negative. And becoming even more wary of it when she said, "It's about myself," though he managed a "Why not?"

"Myself to the age of possibly six months."

He couldn't help smiling at her profile in the dimness, couldn't help saying, "A short story?", which she ignored, in no mood for trivial fun, or not hearing him through what she was thinking, quiet for a time, facing the bouncing light-beams brushing over the forest alongside, the upright trees given a tilt by the slanted road—watching the lights, but as if she might come back to her manuscript any minute.

And he in the silence asking himself What did he make of this girl, this woman?—appealing to him (literally, wanting his help), and in another sense not at all appealing to him; leaving him half annoyed at her persistence, her assurance, and at the same time sympathetic for her concern with this book she had put together. Watching her face, with its features that added up to what in his twenties he would have called pretty but that nowadays suggested an individuality that interested him more—or might, if he asked some everyday questions about her life to bring his information up to the level of hers about him.

Held back from asking, though, by the chance such questions would lead her to think he was more interested in her than he was, would read her book with more interest than he really would; and besides, whatever came of this trip into "the back country" (the "District of Look Behind," she had called it once) he was too old to have it matter much who his companion was. Certainly he was not particularly "drawn" to this one (in his old-fashioned terminology)—too somehow "suspended" for his antique tastes—and yet the touch of her fingers had stayed with him as if they had smudged him with a color. Not as their touch would have done in his twenties but longer than he was prepared for today, since the two seconds, the half-second, that had changed his life, crippled him, left him immune to such touches—and enjoying the immunity in a Pyrrhic sort of way, as he half enjoyed aging for the narrowing space in which disasters had to operate; but hoping, and believing, such immunity would end at the sight of Claudia, swept away in the flood of past images.

And yet he had a liking for these writing people driven to underscore their lives with words as if to reassure their doubts of existing, and he brought up the book again as you might return a pencil you had borrowed. "Your story, don't you think it would be better to finish it first? It's hard enough for a publisher to guess about a novel even when it's finished," saying it partly as good fatherly advice and partly for the possibility such a delay might let him escape reading it altogether—the mention of "story" throwing him back for an instant to the Christmas party and Erik handing out "ballots" for their vote: "Your ballot, madam," to Sarah-Wesley, the mate beside her brushing him away with a word in Norwegian, and, "Would you like to see my School? I have pictures." "Oh, yes I would."—And the vote on the stories never taken—

The woman beside him saying, "It's almost finished," dismissing it, lifting her chin as if listening to the drums, closer now and giving the effect of seeming larger drums, then saying as though she had been thinking of nothing else, "There's no telling what you're going to see, Edward. It's like a scuba dive into another world, that's the same world too." He said the chef seemed to have reservations about their going, and she said, "Oh Hugh Jim! 'Old year dying, new year borning'—what of it! We celebrate New Year's too, don't we? If that's what they're doing," hardly hearing her for the question that often crossed his mind in the presence of almost any woman: Would he want to be married to her? as you might pass a house and wonder if you would like to live there. Usually answered by, Under no circumstances! Also the answer in regard to this one, "attractive" to many, no question, but not to him—the reason too subtle to point to, unless it rested on his own shortcomings.

"Lot and his daughters once, somebody told us, or something remotely like it. Somebody else said it wasn't 'Lot' at all, they never heard of Lot. But 'Old year dying, new year borning,' that's not so far away from Lot and his daughters.''

He said he had forgotten the story of Lot, and she said, ''Oh you remember Lot. Where the older sister said unto the younger, 'Our father is old and there is not a man in the earth to come unto us after the manner of all the earth . . .''' voice trailing off as the car made a sharp turn onto a different surface and shortly stopped in a wider space beside an oxcart with solid wheels and shafts resting on the ground, the wooded slopes beyond it vanishing like sorcery as the driver cut the lights.

And springing out again as he pulled them on in reflex to the sudden voice beyond the cart saying, ''Hold it!'' as a tall man in a sleeveless coral-red shirt moved past the wheels. He and the driver gripped each other's forearm in a fraternal greeting, the driver mumbling what might have been ''Hugh Jim'' and nodding his cap a quarter-inch in their direction, the man motionless for a moment as if to give his thoughts a steady landing-place then holding out the pink flat of his hand in a gesture of ''Wait!'' and disappearing into the trees, the bamboo, the driver close behind him.

Disappearing as if into the drum-sounds, the pounding ornamented now with lacy fluttering slaps breaking the sustained rumble that he seemed to feel as much as hear, a sort of visceral hearing as if his whole body were listening, every hair lifting to listen, the girl moving closer beside him (or he moving closer to her) as if seeking shelter from rain or from wind, or from they hardly knew what, no words between them as though the muttering drums carried words enough—the man reappearing in the orange glow and gesturing behind him, saying nothing, then pressing the light switch and producing darkness like a soft explosion, pitch black about them lined with cracks of light through the bamboo.

They stopped by a tropical tree as if the scene below them demanded a halt, stood for a minute among the spread of exposed roots as if hoping to interpret the drumbeats, then crouched on the side of the slope, gazing down into a clearing in front of a hut, ignored, if noticed at all, by a circle of festively dressed men and women seated crosslegged on the level ground, lanterns before them set in front of metal basins on edge as reflectors, a smoldering fire in the middle mostly ashes seeming to produce no smoke but only wisps of an aromatic scent that he couldn't place, the scent floating up like smoke. Drums in a cluster across from the hut pounding like hearts of strong runners—72 to the minute, brief flutters of 144, then back to 72—bass drums from oil barrels, tenor drums from barrels sawed in half, from trunks of trees. The sudden grip of her hand seemed as much a response to the drums as a need for simple contact, though he wondered if he weren't reading himself into the movement, the touch of her fingers crossing out the years between them, or some of them.

Dancing bodies—young men, young women—all bare-chested, all wrapped in swinging colored skirts corded at the waist, women hardly distinguishable from men except by their young tight breasts, the frailty of their shoulders and the just-offbeat sway of their hips, all shining with sweat in the lantern light and the fire light like wet tin, dancing to the thumping drums and the undulating rope of wordless moaning from the circle—the half-circle—moaning that rose and fell in an up-and-down unfolding rise and fall like the road they had come by, climbing into shrill peaks of sound that fell abruptly into sound-valleys as if crowded over a cliff, the dancers making a drum out of the hard earth with their pounding feet, all of it with an unaccountable feel, for him, of being preparatory, making him think of "Overture," but Overture to a Second or Third Act, as if he had missed the opening, he and his hostess—seated halfway up the slope, elbows on a bed of leaves that were dry but still held a smell of mold suggesting damp earth below, as what they saw seemed laid on much they didn't see, only felt, only smelled, the dancers moving to the rhythm of the slapping hands, the moaning, the almost-singing, girl breasts swinging just out of cadence like alto voices under soprano.

Then a lull in the moaning, the drums only murmuring, and two youths leading out of the hut a frail and ancient man in a striped robe to his bare feet and seating him gently in a weathered wicker chair with a high back as if presenting the High Priest of the ritual (or Gran Met himself!), the drums suddenly silent in a sort of reversed fanfare, the dancers still, motionless in a half-circle facing the chair, the throne.

The whole of it resolving for him into an impulsive need to touch this young half-his-age body beside him; that moved against him as if on the swell of the same wave, he leaning across her and kissing her stranger's mouth, reminded of Claudia by the river and the gallery of memories she moved in like a shadow among the light-dark-light images in front of him, in front of them. She whispering, "Lot?" in a question, and after a moment, "'And the first born said unto the younger, Come, let us make our father drink wine and we will lie with him, that we may preserve the seed of our father . . . .'"

"Take a drink, Mr. First Mate; you're not having any fun." And, "Would you like to see my School? I have pictures." "Oh, yes I would."—Ray hesitating (no concern of his), then following them, uneasy at the misread signals.

The mate snapping the lock on the door with a firmness that seemed to alarm her. "Don't lock the door,'' quietly and with maybe a teetering smile but her voice subtly different, a change of pitch, the same key as the ''Oh, yes I would'' but a quarter-tone lower as if striking a wall and coming back distorted. A hurried, ''I can't stay but a minute,'' no longer the life of the party, a looking-behind-her voice, the words clear enough through the dance music filling the corridor outside, as if she were standing near the ventilator slats in the door, the mate speaking some words with a new authority and she raising her voice and calling out something, and the Captain's voice in the narrow passageway drowning out the music with, ''Open the door, Wagman!'' as he shook the doorknob, then with, ''This is your captain!'' then with, ''Stand clear!'' and the corridor full to bursting with the pistol ball into the lock, the door swinging free on Sarah-Wesley hugging her bare chest and the mate motionless in a far corner eyes on the deck . . . .

And the old man motionless, until moving to lift a hand and seeming to lift the voice sounds, and the drum sounds lifting in a brushing whisper that seemed a cue to the dancers, to two of them, both stepping out of their skirts and striding into the fire-glow on elegant tan moves of pink-soled feet, the glow and lantern-light in streaks and shadows on sweating skin, the old man raising his eyes as the drums came up from whisper to mumble, the girls moving in tune with the drum notes and the voice notes over the drums like birds sailing, the girl beside Ray—what was her name?—moving against him, or he against her, laying a hand on his chest and gripping his when he touched it, the unknown hand of a stranger immediately familiar as if joined to his by what they were seeing.

The dancers in front of the chair now, turning away from each other in separated patterns that faced the old man with the moving buttocks of one and the moving belly of the other as they turned on close-together feet, the arms of both in a continuous weave of forearms and wrists and fingers out of India or the East, though he felt the heritage more than thought it, all thinking subdued as if by the drums and the chanting that seemed to spread feeling in place of thinking, he and the girl

("Janet," of course) as if dreaming the same dream from opposite parts of the night, he the old man, she the naked dancers—as they turned in sweating scrolls and moved closer to the chair and one of them dropped on a knee and lifted aside the hem of the striped robe, parted his spindly shanks and brushed a hand up the inside of his thigh, twirling away on a rise in the drum beats and a rise of the voices in acclamation, Janet's hand under Ray's freeing itself and repeating-echoing-trasposing what she had just seen, or just imagined.

And he hardly knowing which awareness-level he himself was in, removed by her touch from his cripple-world as in dreams he ran with young forgotten legs, heard long-silent voices in long-silent tones, doubts, uncertainties, apathies discarded like everyday necessities abandoned in a hurried escape—two shrunken old women appearing past the drums, hardly visible under the loads of palm fronds bunched in their arms, laying them out before the hut, smoothing them, patting the edges in a housekeeperly way as if making a bed, one end on the step of the hut and higher than the other, two of the young men guiding the old one, solicitously steering him, settling him at his length on the sloping bed; one of the dancers dropping beside him, breasts flattened against drawn-up knees, fingers on the two pipes of a bamboo flute attached to one mouthpiece that she coaxed into a monotonous four or five notes Ray could hardly hear for the distance and the envelope of drum sounds, trilling them, aiming them, at the center of the old man's legs as if he had been a dervish's basket with a sleeping cobra, the center beginning to stir as the old man stared past her at the other dancers moving to the notes as though translating sound into motion, heads slightly turned, eyes chastely on the stomped earth to one side of their steps but lifting them now and then to the old man as if measuring his watching them from where he lay, the old man seeming to watch the dark V at the fork of their legs as you sometimes watch the speaking lips of someone instead of the eyes, one of the dancers, as she neared him, sinking to her knees and throwing a leg over him as if he had been the saddle of a motorcycle, settling herself, grasping his upper arms for handlebars, the chanting voices rising as if in response and the drum sounds rising.

And Ray in his antique propriety half prepared for the woman beside him to spring to her feet and run away from it up the slope, not prepared for her moving against him reflecting the girl, moving expertly over him, his mind for an instant with the other soft shelf and the fisherman wading past their held breaths, held-back laughs; then forgetting the long-ago, forgetting the old man, the girl with the old man between her legs, discarding them as you discard a pattern you know by heart, or fusing the two old men, the two young women, all four rising in transports like the voices, the chanting, like the drums—like the pigeon tossed into the air by someone in the circle, lifting away and gone; as he himself seemed lifted away over distance and time and blankness to his hotel bed under the lazy fan, the early sun slanting across the Park into his window, all of it unreal except the feeling in himself of opening his eyes on a day of sharper sun and shade, and the pillow by his head under an airy scent of jasmin, and the note by the ashtray on a table that he held in the sunlight and read without glasses: *MS at desk, or soon will be. J. — Lunch?* Or was it, *"Love"?* No, *"Lunch",* setting no store by intimacy (in their modern throw-it-away decorum), trading the weight of her narrow body on his chest for a reader, and maybe, who could tell?, a publisher; that she wouldn't know in daylight walking toward her on the street.

The *"MS"* brought up to him while he was shaving by a boy in a white coat with sleeves to his knuckles, "J. Tyner" with a firm pen in a corner of the envelope, "P.O.Box 763, Davistown, S. Juan de Pinos" when he found his glasses. Not very heavy, he was glad to think, through thoughts already putting together the editor note he would enclose, ". . . you write with warmth and an appealing spontaneity" (extrapolating). "Suggest you complete . . . novels sometimes hard to evaluate even when completed. Will bear it in mind in case I hear . . . ."

No. No. He was too out-of-date to be able to dismiss intensities so lightly—except that their very intensities contributed to making them dismissable for him, as his ears with their deficiencies welcomed *legato* over *allegretto*; as his scales weighed felicity over delight, devotion over prurience. Weighed highest what Stevens called love's celestial ease in the heart—the words sending him once more to the phone in the lobby and the voice he had heard before giving much the same answer: "Miss Claudia is expected for lunch at two, is there a message?"

"Thank you, no message."

"If you will leave your name, sir, . . ."

"Thank you, I'll call later."

And he walked out onto the high porch to the semi-British breakfast served to him on the broad flat arm of the chair she had sat in the night before—fresh pineapple, scones with sultanas, grilled something or other that might have been turtle or shark or eel in place of kipper—the chair and the Park and the *22 Taxis Facing West* (two this morning, neither one theirs) all but invisible beyond a screen of bamboo and vines and tree trunks, and the black bodies swaying in the lantern light, and the pliant soft chest against his own that was strange and familiar too, all of it like a tune that gets hung in your head and can only be quieted by another tune to displace it.

Which "Some more coffee, sir?" almost was,

bringing with it a reminder of the regal boxes of Havana cigars he had seen in the lobby, and while the waiter cleared the dishes from the chair arm he found and lit a *Larranaga cetro* such as he hadn't luxuriated in for decades, returned to the chair, put his feet on the banister American style and pulled out the manuscript from the envelope—to read the usual first three pages, a middle three, perhaps the last three, depending on the others (never able to approach a new manuscript without hearing the rusty quip of, probably, a white-waistcoated editor of *The Atlantic* that "One needn't eat the whole egg to know that it's bad").

"AUTOBIOGRAPHY OF A BABE IN ARMS"—Well? Hhm. Maybe yes, maybe no (Carbon copy. Holding back the original? Or having already sent it to New York? Multiple submission, even in one so young? A fast learner.)

Call me Penelope, Penny, if you like. A weaver. I also answer to Augusta named for the month I began. . . .

And after a scoop of fading pages (carbon paper wearing thin, new sheet—a firmer voice):

. . . stopping the car and leading her to the bank of a rushing mountain river at a place he seemed to know about (from other times, perhaps?) and giving her a hand down a sloping bank to a leafy shelf, talking all the while as if to cover his designs, or hoping to. Shoes off, socks into shoes with a fussy neatness, cotton pants rolled up over legs with the hair worn off on the backs like the haunches of a moldy deer in a small-town zoo, cringing from the cold water as he waded in, this man she hardly knew, turning round, begging, "Come on, come on."

"I'm not coming in."

"Come on, you'll like it."

Goosebumps on her calves, the backs of her knees, her thighs as she bunched up her skirt and waded in, the water off a snow peak or seeming so, a glacier, wading in a step or two, searching for a good excuse to leave, escape, without seeming priggish to this persistent all-but-stranger. Refusing his held-out hand, pushing it away, when she slipped on the slime of an underwater rock, both of them turning to look downstream at a sound or something moving and seeing a stout fisherman emerging at a bend in glistening boots, casting, reeling in, looping his line and casting again, absorbed, as if the world depended on where it fell, and both of them splashing to the bank and up to the shelf behind the limbs and lying there still as puzzled squirrels. . . .

Hair trying to stand on end, shoes thumping down off the banister, two-inch cultivated ash lost off the cigar, his "Just a minute now!" meant for himself but tumbling out strong enough to bring a "Yes sir?" from the boy who had delivered the pages, or his double. Ray waving him off with the pages themselves, mumbling to himself that stranger things had happened (and trying to think of one), arguing it was not so strange after all for her to imagine two people wading in a stream on a hot day, even hiding on the bank from an intrusive fisherman; there were such mountain streams, such days, such fishermen on the Island at her doorstep.—Glad he was able to revive the cigar, the aroma itself reassuring.

Another scoop of pages, fading out then black (new carbon), and:

. . . she told him not to wait, please not to wait, there under the four-sided moon-clock creeping up on midnight and train time, this man who had followed her to New York—inventing all sorts of odd reasons, not telling her he was coming then phoning he was there "on business"; this man whose invitations she had refused all week suddenly walking up beside her as she handed her ticket to the fatherly man in blue at the table by the gate. "I can manage, John. Please don't wait."

"You've been avoiding me."

"Avoiding you, what do you mean?" smiling a thank-you to the blue-coated man returning what was left of her ticket—smiling to show she could smile if she cared to—putting the ticket-stub away in her handbag and closing the catch with a firm snap that she meant as dismissal to this insistent reappearing John Somebody.

"I mean avoiding me."

"Good-by, John. Please don't wait, I can manage—what are you doing!" as he laid a green ticket on the table.

"I happen to be on this train too."

"You what!" surprise going into anger, into something close to fury.

"Doctor's appointment in Baltimore tomorrow."

Wordless, and holding herself rigid to draw a deep breath into her chest then expel it with, "You don't look sick," and as he handed a porter the check for his luggage and some money and pointed at the checkroom, "You don't act sick either," voice as stinging as she could make it.

"Oh I'm not. Just routine."

She studying him a minute in the dozing hum of the midnight station that floated down like snow, then turning away and hurrying through the gate and down the steps to the black train . . . .

Throwing the cigar over the banister at the *22 Taxis Facing West,* crossing the porch at a stumble until he remembered to take off his glasses, scribbling, "Emergency call from home office. Thanks for showing this to me. Will write" on a hotel pad at the desk and sliding it in with the manuscript. "My bill, please. And please hand this to Mrs. Tyner when she calls."

"Leaving, sir? Anything wrong, sir?"

Assuring the clerk of the hotel's excellence and asking about planes for the United States, the clerk running his finger down a schedule by the letter boxes and reporting a non-stop flight to Miami at "thirteen thirty-seven," both of them glancing at the clock over the boxes showing five minutes to eleven.

"Would you send somebody for my bags? And please get me a taxi," (not No. 17, please God),—a long wait at the terminal, but rather that than being at the hotel when she came for the manuscript, pushing the envelope across the counter with the tips of his fingers as if it might explode, hadn't exploded.

"Very good, sir. Have nice fly."

"Thank you," turning away, then facing back. "Tell me, you know Mrs. Tyner, do you happen to know Mrs. Tyner's name before she married?"

"Oh, sorry, sir," with a little smile at the impropriety of such a question, then indulgently, "Perhaps our Social Director—but she doesn't come on until noon."

But there were other questions that haunted him as he waited in his bolted-down chair before the two-way mirror-window—shining white planes beyond it slanting past with the soft hum of muted cellos, slanting up, slanting down, slicing through the travelers at his back, the hatted and the hatless, the restless and the patient, through a barefoot boy with a dog on a leash, through the hand luggage, the carry-on, through the dancers turning on the powdered earth, the chanting, the resurrected old man (old men!), through the questions pounding in his head like the drums: who was this woman, this girl? calling herself Augusta, "named for the month I began," counting back from a birthday and coming to his month in the mountains? Or told by her mother she "began" in the month of August? Her embittered mother?

Or was it all just fiction, just a putting

together of stories she had heard, fancies she had dreamed, like any other of those strange people at their writing machines? She might never have heard the name, Claudia Motlow—

The mirror-window becoming all window, the bowed trunks of the two palms sliced off by the waiting-room ceiling, the herringbone path between the sprinklers filled with passengers out of the sky, with welcomes that reached from restrained to exuberant, from handshakes to open arms, and in the midst of the animated parade to the waiting room and his bolted-down chair Janet in white and yellow arm-in-arm with a woman his age (nearly), black hair now a well-kept gray, well-made navy blue linen skirt and jacket with the, for him, indefinable something that said taste, if not hers then some knowing saleswoman's in a costly shop. If he moved he would draw their attention, after a moment would be hearing, "Mother" (probably, "Mum," or, "Mom"), "this is Edward—what did you say your name was? King?" "Ray. Edward Ray. Aren't you confusing me with Oedipus the King? . . ."

If he held his breath, pulled in his shoulders, turned his face slowly, very slowly, away to watch the barefoot boy behind him and the dog, sat as still as a puzzled squirrel—